D1580285

COMRADES
IN ARMS

STORIES OF

'BIGGLES' of the R·A·F, 'WORRALS' of the W·A·A·F
and 'KING' of the Commandos

"GIMLET"

Captain Lorrington King, D.S.O. M.C.

COMRADES
IN ARMS

STORIES OF

'BIGGLES' of the R·A·F· 'WORRALS' of the W·A·A·F·
and 'KING' of the Commandos

by

CAPTAIN
W.E.JOHNS

Illustrated by
Stead

London HODDER & STOUGHTON Limited

*The characters in this book are entirely imaginary and
have no relation to any living persons*

First printed August, 1947

*Printed in Great Britain for Hodder & Stoughton Ltd., London
by Ebenezer Baylis & Son Ltd., The Trinity Press, Worcester
and London*

CONTENTS

STORY

I

AN ORIENTAL ASSIGNMENT

A "King" Of The Commandos Story

CORPORAL ALBERT COLLSON, commonly called "Copper" from the fact of his once having been a member of the Metropolitan Police Force, walked with confidence into the recreation room of the Special Service Troop of Combined Operations known in places where fighting men meet, as "King's Kittens"— this familiar and quite inappropriate name being derived from the cypher, a wildcat, worn on the shoulders. His eyes made a quick survey and came to rest on two men—or rather, a man and a youth—who sat alone at a small table sipping coffee. The man was slim, swarthy, and sported a tiny black moustache on a face that would have been good-looking had it not been mutilated by a scar, a souvenir handed out by a grizzly when he, "Trapper" Troublay, a French Canadian, had been in fact a trapper in the North West Territory of the Dominion. There was nothing remarkable about his companion, Nigel Peters, otherwise "Cub," apart from his extreme youth in relation to the uniform he wore. His face was rather thin, perhaps, and set in hard

7

lines, the result of looking upon death too often when, some time earlier, he had been a refugee in occupied France.

Copper crossed the room and halted by the table, his six feet two inches of brawn and muscle towering above it. "Still chin-wagging," he bantered. "Beats me what you two find to jaw about, s'welp me. Get on your pins; the Skipper's waiting to see us in the office."

Trapper glanced up, interest lighting his dark eyes. "Something cooking?" he questioned.

"Gimlet ain't likely ter send fer us to ask how we like our eggs boiled," returned Copper sarcastically. "Get mobile."

The three commandos left the room, crossed the square and came to a halt in front of a door bearing the notice in white letters: Captain Lorrington King, D.S.O., M.C. Copper knocked. A voice called, "Come in." Copper thrust the door open, took three quick short paces, stiffened to attention and saluted. "Party all present, sir," he announced.

Captain King, known affectionately to the men who served under him as "Gimlet," glanced up from a desk on which was spread a map. "All right. Sit down you fellows," he said quietly. "Smoke if you want to."

Copper pulled a chair forward and sat down. The others did the same. Trapper lit a cigarette.

It was a minute or two before Gimlet spoke. He looked up, and resting his chin on clenched hands, elbows on the desk, considered the trio before him with eyes so blue and bright that no defaulter had ever been able to meet them. "We've been asked to do a little job," he said, in the soft, modulated tone of voice sometimes known as "Oxford." "It should be easy—

8

quite easy. Might turn out to be good fun. The only thing is, the theatre of operations is rather a long way off. Still, we shall fly out, so it may not be too bad. Any of you know a place called Indo-China?"

Copper shook his head. "No, sir. Never 'eard of it."

Trapper looked blank. "Nor me, sir."

Cub spoke up. "You mean the French colony beyond Burma and Siam now occupied by the Japanese?"

"That's right," replied Gimlet, looking down at his map.

Copper nudged Cub, who was sitting next to him, with an elbow. "You know a sight too much," he breathed. "What's the idea? Are you after my stripes?"

Gimlet looked at Copper. "Did you say something, corporal?"

Copper cleared his throat. "No, sir."

"Sorry," murmured Gimlet. "I thought you spoke. Now pay attention," he went on. "The people who live in this country where we are going are mostly Chinese, but the place being a French colony, French is the official language. It is on account of our know-ledge of French—excluding Copper—that we have been detailed for this particular raid. Make yourselves comfortable while I run over the general scheme. I'll make it as short as possible, but it will take a little while. In a nutshell, according to our orders, we're going to the East to collect, and bring home, an unusual form of *Hevea braziliensis*.

Copper looked startled. "I wouldn't trust a man with a name like that, sir," he asserted positively. "Do I have to remember it?"

Gimlet did not smile. "*Hevea braziliensis* is the

botanical name of the tree from which is derived the stuff we call india-rubber."

Copper looked relieved, but still doubtful. "So we're goin' ter bring 'ome a tree, eh?"

"No," answered Gimlet. "We're going to bring home the seeds of a tree. And now, if you'll refrain from comment until I've finished, I'll run over the story." Gimlet took a cigarette from a gold case, and having lighted it, continued.

"One of the greatest living horticultural experts is, or was, an Englishman by the name of Sir Lionel Radnor. He has, by cross-breeding, produced several new fruits and vegetables. Some years ago he went to the East at the request of the British government with the object of developing or breeding a form of rubber plant of sufficient hardiness to be grown in a temperate climate. The object of this was in case we should ever lose Malaya, the greatest rubber producing country in the world—and this, as you know, has actually happened—we should be able to grow rubber sufficient for our needs in the event of war. The idea was, I believe, to grow this new rubber in Canada, if a tree could be found hardy enough to stand the climate. All this, of course, was to be done in secret. Well, Sir Lionel was successful in his quest. In the Yunnan province of Western China he found, and developed, a dwarf, hardy, fast-growing form of rubber plant. The seeds which he would have brought home were just ripening when the Japanese struck at us. The seeds, as they were then, not being ripe, were useless; so with great courage he decided to wait for them to finish ripening, when, with luck, he would get them home. Unfortunately his luck was out. The seeds ripened. He put twenty of them, sufficient for stock, in a tin, destroyed the rest, and with his chief native assistant, a Chinese named Charla Song, started for India. He was caught whilst crossing Indo-China. The Japs, not knowing the importance of the man they had got hold of, took him to Saigon; for Sir Lionel was clever enough to persuade them that he was a Frenchman willing to collaborate with them. He was determined to get home at any cost. But in Saigon he was recognized, and the game was up. At the time he had been permitted to live in the Oriente Hotel, and he was actually in the reading-room there when he was warned by a native that the Japs had learned who he was, and soldiers were on the way to take him into custody. Sir Lionel's first thoughts were for his precious seeds, for he realized that should they fall into enemy hands it would be a disaster of the first magnitude. True, the Japs, having seized Malaya, were not short of rubber; but should they acquire the seeds, they would, after the war, be able to develop a rubber industry of their own, which would ruin the British planters in Malaya. All this he perceived very clearly. Yet, naturally, he was loath to destroy the fruits of years of labour; so he looked around for some place to hide the seeds. He found one. In a niche in the wall —he was still in the reading-room of the Oriente Hotel —there stood a carved ebony elephant, with its trunk upraised. It was hollow. Down the hollow trunk Sir Lionel dropped the twenty seeds, one by one, so that they fell into the body of the beast. He had just completed this operation when the Japs arrived and arrested him. He was taken to Japan. There, soon afterwards, the Japs learned—probably through their Intelligence service—of Sir Lionel's real mission in the East. They asked him what he had done with the seeds. This information he refused to give, whereupon he was tortured so horribly that he died." Gimlet stubbed his cigarette and lit another.

"In these circumstances you will be wondering how we came by this information," he resumed. "I mentioned just now Sir Lionel's loyal and devoted assistant, Charla Song. He managed to evade the Japs, and somehow or other kept in touch with his chief until Sir Lionel was taken to Japan. It was from Charla Song that we got the story, although not directly, because he, for reasons of his own, elected to remain in Saigon. Instead of trying to get through to us in person he entrusted the secret to a Burmese who, months later, after a terrible journey, managed to make contact with the Fourteenth Army then advancing through Upper Burma. That, briefly, is the story. Of course, any thing can have happened in the meantime, but the government thinks there is a good chance that the seeds may still be in the ebony elephant in the Oriente Hotel. We are going to Saigon to find out. If we can get the seeds home, so well and good; if not, we are to destroy them to prevent them from falling into the hands of the enemy—always assuming, of course, that the seeds are still where Sir Lionel hid them."

"But if the Japs know of the existence of these seeds, and apparently they do, surely the first place they would search would be the Oriente Hotel?" remarked Cub.

"That is a perfectly natural conclusion," answered Gimlet. "I said something to the same effect to the Intelligence officer who told me the story. But it seems that if the Japs did search the Oriente they did not find the seeds, because long after the affair at Saigon they took the trouble to ransack the bungalow which

Sir Lionel had occupied whilst carrying out his experiments. In fact, they pulled the place down piece by piece. They could only have been looking for the seeds. Hence, we may assume that they had not found them—not at that time, anyway."

"There were no bushes with any more seeds on at the bungalow, I hope?" put in Copper shrewdly.

"Sir Lionel and Charla Song took care of that," asserted Gimlet. "They cut every bush to the ground before they left."

"*Tch!* So these twenty seeds are the only ones in the world?" muttered Trapper.

"They are," confirmed Gimlet. "Consequently they are worth a good deal more than their weight in gold or diamonds. In fact, they are worth so much to British post-war industry that the government is prepared to go to any lengths to recover them—or to prevent anyone else from obtaining them. If we get the seeds, should there be the slightest chance of our being captured by the Japs, we are to destroy them instantly."

"When do we start on this jaunt, sir?" asked Copper.

"To-morrow morning," replied Gimlet. "We shall fly straight out to Calcutta, which will be our base for the operation. From there a long-range flying-boat, a Catalina, will fly us at night across Lower Burma to the Gulf of Siam and drop us somewhere just off the southern tip of Cochin China. Carrying iron rations we shall go ashore in a rubber dinghy, which we shall hide in the forest, and then go on, on foot, to Saigon. The flying-boat, which would of course be seen in the hours of daylight, will return home."

"And what about us, sir? How do we get home?" asked Copper anxiously.

13

"The Catalina will return to the rendezvous every second day. If we show a signal it will land and pick us up. If, after fourteen days, no signal light is seen, the boat will abandon the project and we shall be posted as missing, believed killed," said Gimlet imperturbably.

"And I reckon there won't be no lie about that," averred Copper grimly. "Do we go in these togs?"

"Only as far as Calcutta. There we shall be provided with garments more suitable for the occasion. When we get on enemy territory, if we are seen—and we certainly shall be—we shall have to pass as French."

Copper looked dubious. "What a hope I've got," he said morosely. "Looks as if I'm goin' ter be in the way, sir."

"Not at all," returned Gimlet. "One of our difficulties will be food. To save awkward situations we shall have to take with us all that we are likely to need. Someone will have to carry it; and as a bulky parcel might arouse curiosity in Saigon we shall have to make a dump somewhere. A dump will need someone to look after it—if necessary, fight to protect it. That's a job you should be able to do very well, corporal.' '

"If you say so, sir," agreed Copper.

"I have been able to arrange one detail that relieves my mind as far as transport is concerned," went on Gimlet. "We shall have one of the most experienced pilots in the service; the officer who has twice flown us home from France when things were looking distinctly gloomy."

"You mean Squadron Leader Bigglesworth, sir?" queried Cub.

Gimlet nodded. "The Higher Command fixed it with the Air Ministry."

14

"That's something, anyway," murmured Copper.

"On a show like this, to have a pilot one can rely on is more than something," corrected Gimlet softly. "It's almost everything. Squadron Leader Bigglesworth will provide his own air crew. Well, I think that's all. You fellows had better get some sleep. We parade in the morning at four-thirty outside this office."

Copper rose and saluted. "Aye aye, sir."

"Just one last point, corporal," added Gimlet.

"Yes sir."

"Your hair is getting long again. Better get it cut before we start; it may be some time before you get another chance."

Copper swallowed hard. "Very good, sir." He went out, closed the door, and leaned against the wall, a hand over his eyes. "Sufferin' barnacles!" he groaned. "Did you hear that? Get me 'air cut. Anyone would think we was goin' to a bunfight at Buckingham Palace, s'welp me. Blimy! What a life!"

II

Cub raised himself from the reclining position into which he had sunk as at long last the monotonous purr of the Catalina's engines, throttled back to cruising speed, died, giving way after more than six hours of unbroken life to a strange uneasy silence. He looked out through the side window, but there was little to be seen. Above, a sky spangled with a million stars, not stuck on the flat face of heaven as they appear to be in northern climes, but hanging low in a dome so vast that it embraced the universe. The moon had not yet risen. Far below, a vague unbroken shadow, as

15

devoid of movement as an icebound pool, marked the surface of the Gulf of Siam. On all sides it rolled away and away to merge at last into the pitiless distance. The hull of the big flying boat tilted gently towards the bows.

"We must be getting somewhere at last," remarked Copper. "About time too. I was just a'thinkin' that if we went on much longer we should be back where we started from. We're gettin' a sight too far from 'ome fer my likin', and no bloomin' error."

Gimlet appeared forward from the control cabin where he had been in conference with the captain of the aircraft, Squadron Leader Bigglesworth. Cub smiled at his appearance, although as they were all dressed practically alike, in rather soiled civilian suits of tropical khaki drill, with straw or panama hats, there was really little to laugh at. They looked, as Copper had aptly remarked, like part of a broken-down concert party.

"We're nearly there," announced Gimlet curtly. "The machine is losing height. Stand by to move smartly as soon as we are on the water. The captain doesn't want to hang about so near hostile country longer than is necessary."

"No one's likely to blame him for that," murmured Copper in a low voice, as he reached out for the heavy kit bag which contained iron rations for fourteen days, this being his personal responsibility.

Still losing height, the Catalina began to turn in wide flat circles and continued doing so for some minutes. The forward bulkhead door opened and a cheerful-faced ginger-haired flying officer came in. "We're almost on the water," said he. "Cape Cambodia is straight ahead. We daren't go nearer than four miles on account of the noise of our engines; but the current is running right for you and you should make your landfall well before dawn." He looked at his watch. "My skipper wants us to synchronize our watches so that there won't be any mistake about the time when we return. It is now sixteen minutes past three."

As the commandos checked their watches the aircraft came back to level flight, and a moment later a long liquid *swish* announced that the keel was cutting the surface of the gulf. The aircraft rocked gently as it came to rest. The ginger-headed flying officer opened the cabin door and looked out. "Lovely night, sea dead calm and nothing in sight," he announced. "What more could you ask for?"

"A nice return ticket to 'ampstead 'eath," answered Copper promptly, bending his back to the task of launching the dinghy, an operation which, with the loading of rations and equipment, occupied the next ten minutes. The little craft was then pushed clear and paddles taken in hand.

"Good luck, boys," said the captain of the flying boat from the cabin door. "See you here, same spot, same time, Wednesday morning."

"We hope," breathed Copper.

Gimlet raised a hand in a parting salutation. "Cheer-ho, Biggles. Don't forget what I said about the shooting down at Lorrington should any of your boys feel like a day's sport. There aren't as many birds as there should be, but my keeper says there should be thirty brace in the long wood."

"I'll remember it, thanks," came the reply.

Copper nudged Cub. "There they go again," he groaned in a broken whisper. "'Ere we are, likely to be shot at any minute, and what do they talk about?

Dicky birds. S'welp me, it's enough the break the 'eart of a brass monkey."

"Not so much talking there," ordered Gimlet curtly.

"Aye, aye, sir," sighed Copper.

Paddles dipped, and the little craft began to move towards a long black shadow that formed the northern horizon. Behind the dinghy the disturbed water glowed with dull phosphorescent fire. The outline of the flying boat became indistinct as, with engines purring, it taxied seaward before opening up for the take-off. Slowly the black shadow of the land hardened, and Gimlet paused more often to survey it through his night glasses. In an hour the silhouette of motionless palms cut a delicate tracery in a sky paling in the light of a rising moon.

"This is the tricky bit," whispered Gimlet. "If we've been spotted they'll open fire as we step ashore. If that happens there can be no question of going back; it will be every man for himself."

The dinghy crept on towards a long shelving strip of sand. The only sound was the soft swish of paddles and the murmur of tiny wavelets dying on the beach. The little craft faltered and came to a stop as its bottom grated gently on the sand. Gimlet stood up and stepped out into six inches of water. For a few seconds he stood there, staring, listening; then he turned and whispered: "All clear. Let's get the boat up."

The small vessel was lifted bodily and carried up into the jungle that backed the beach. Copper, under Gimlet's orders, using a fallen palm frond as a brush, erased the footprints in the sand, while the others, with more fronds and dead leaves, covered the boat so that it could not be seen. Gimlet noted the spot carefully and made the others do the same.

18

"The next thing is to get to the road," he said quietly. "According to my map it runs parallel with the beach about half a mile inland. We shan't get to Saigon to-night, of course; it's twenty miles away; but we'll push on as far as possible while darkness holds. As soon as it starts to get light we must look for a suitable place to hide up, where we can discuss the plan I have in mind. Come on. Bring the bag, corporal. Single file. No more talking." He set off through the jungle away from the sea.

A rather difficult march of twenty minutes through dense forest brought the party to the road. A cautious reconnaissance having revealed that it was deserted the march was continued, now in easy going, and in this order some five or six miles were covered before the rays of the rising sun brought Gimlet to a halt.

"I've been on the look-out, but so far I haven't seen anything suitable for a dump," he remarked. "We shall soon have to find somewhere, but I think we might risk going on for a bit. Keep close to the trees and dive for cover should anyone appear."

It was broad daylight before they found a hiding-place which Gimlet considered suitable for their purpose. Copper called it a house, but it was hardly that. It was, in fact, a palm-thatched hut in the last stages of dilapidation some thirty yards from the road and half buried in rioting undergrowth; however, it retained the remnant of a roof, and the crumbling walls offered better cover than bushes, so after they had tidied the place up somewhat, an operation enlivened by the sudden appearance of a disturbed cobra which eventually escaped into the jungle, they prepared to make themselves as comfortable as the circumstances permitted. There was no question of lighting a fire to make tea, so plain water and biscuits had to suffice for breakfast. Copper volunteered to take the first watch. He took up a position near what had once been a window, from where he could command a view of the road in both directions.

Gimlet studied his map for a little while in silence. Then he looked up. "Pay attention everybody," he ordered. "Now that we are on the spot I'll run over the details of the scheme I have in mind so that should I become a casualty the rest of you will know what I was doing. You will, of course, carry on. You know the rendezvous with the aircraft and the times it will show up, so one of you at least ought to get through. As you know, our purpose here is definite. All we have to do is collect twenty seeds, about the size of peas, from the Oriente Hotel. The hotel is in the Place Dumont. The Place Dumont is in the centre of the town and the road we are on will take us straight to it. The hotel is an important one so there should be no difficulty in finding it. There is one snag, though. It happens to be the billet of two men either of whom would probably resent our intrusion if our presence became known. One is General Onatishu, the Japanese Commandant of the region, and the other is Monsieur Laffon, the head of the French quisling government here."

Copper stared at Gimlet for a moment in pained surprise. Then he shook his head sadly. "I ought to 'ave known there was a catch in it," he said bitterly.

"I don't see that it need make any difference to our procedure," went on Gimlet dispassionately. "Indeed,

20

the occupation of the hotel by these two men should make it all the safer from our point of view, in that they would hardly expect enemy agents to be so ill-advised as to call on them, so to speak."

"Neither would I—my oath I wouldn't," breathed Copper.

"When I need your opinion, corporal, I'll ask for it," said Gimlet crisply. "Now about travelling," he went on. "A number of people together, even a small party, is apt to attract attention in an occupied country. It would therefore be inadvisable for us to troop up the road in a bunch. I have decided therefore that you, corporal, as you do not speak French, will remain here to take care of the dump and cover our retreat should we return somewhat hurriedly, as is not unlikely. The rest of us will leave here at nine o'clock so as to arrive in the Place Dumont about noon, the hour when most people will be having lunch, or resting out of the heat. I shall walk ahead with Cub. Trapper, you will follow on, keeping about fifty yards in the rear. From that position you should be able to observe if we are followed, or watched. You may also be able to help us if we get into difficulties. When we enter the hotel take up a position near the entrance and keep your eyes open. If we are questioned we shall say we are French planters from the interior. Now for the hotel. I have been provided with a sketch plan obtained by Intelligence from a man who knows the place well. We enter through swing doors into a large vestibule with the bureau on the left and a dining-room on the right. The dining-room doors are usually left open. There will probably be quite a number of people in it taking lunch—Japanese naval and military officers, among others, no doubt. The reading-room, which is our objective, is on the first floor. The door faces the head of the stairway which starts in the vestibule so we should have no difficulty in finding it."

"Suppose there are people in the reading-room?" put in Cub.

"There may be, but the chances are that it will be empty at the time of our visit because most people in the hotel will be at lunch—or they should be. Anyhow, that's a chance we shall have to take. I have of course considered taking a bedroom at the hotel with the object of visiting the reading-room during the night; and it may come to that yet; but the plan raises difficulties, such as the booking of the room at the office and perhaps providing evidence of identification, which may lead to embarrassing questions. We'll try the simple way first. I don't think it's any use planning beyond that at the moment. Everything will depend on conditions as we find them at the hotel." Gimlet smiled. "It may be that we shall be able to walk straight in, collect the seeds, and walk out again, with no questions asked; in which case I should divide the seeds among us so that some of them should get home, anyway."

Trapper grunted, a habit he had caught from Indian companions at home. "*Ma foi!* That's how she works in the story books," he remarked. "I would not bet she will work out like that with us."

"You never said a truer word, chum," observed Copper moodily. "I've never seen an operation yet that worked out according to plan, although according to the papers they always do."

"Maybe this will be the occasion," said Gimlet cheerfully. "Think how dull soldiering would be if everything worked out just as it should go."

22

"It 'ud make a nice change, anyhow," muttered Copper.

Gimlet looked at his watch. "Time we were getting along," he announced. "You lie low here, corporal. Expect us back when you see us. With luck we might be back by nightfall."

"Ha! The soldier who counts on luck should be discharged medically unfit," opined Copper grimly. He stiffened. "Hold hard, sir. Someone's coming."

The others joined him at the window. At first nothing could be seen, but the tramp of marching feet could be heard. Then into view came a file of five Japanese soldiers, one, an N.C.O., marching a little ahead. The men marched carelessly, talking and smoking, obviously on a routine patrol with no danger apprehended. In a few minutes they were out of sight.

"We could have mopped up that bunch as easy as winkin'," declared Copper in a disappointed voice.

"We're not an invasion force," reminded Gimlet shortly. "Our business is to get home without starting anything. That patrol probably passes here about the same time every morning. We shall all do well to remember it. Come on, Cub, let's be moving."

III

Cub's dominant impression of Saigon was heat; suffocating heat. He arrived dripping with perspiration. Apart from that the journey had been comparatively uneventful. Not until they had left the cool shade of the forest and emerged on the open road, which happened at a point about half way, had he any idea of the heat of the direct rays of the sun. Not that Gimlet set a fast pace, for this, he held, might

23

attract attention to them. They strolled rather than marched.

It was some time before they saw anyone. The first person was a jaded-looking white man who was doing something in a garden. He nodded and murmured a brief *bon jour*. Soon afterwards they encountered a Japanese soldier, half dressed, dawdling, apparently off duty. He said nothing. After that there were occasional slant-eyed natives of the peasant class, doing various tasks without enthusiasm. At the approaches of the big town, however, there was an increasing volume of traffic, both pedestrian and vehicular—Japanese service cars, bicycles, rickshaws, cattle, and a miscellaneous assortment of humanity. Gimlet held on through untidy streets flaunting meaningless trade signs and names until, towards the centre of the town, French began to supplant the Chinese symbols. Japanese officers and other ranks also became more numerous. Quite a number of white men, dressed like themselves in tropical kit, were moving about, and for this reason no doubt their progress was not questioned. It was twenty past twelve when Gimlet halted in front of a pretentious building which bore the name, conspicuously displayed on its façade, Hotel Oriente. "Here we are," he breathed.

Cub knew that had he been alone he would have hesitated, as a diver hesitates on a high board, before entering a building which he found rather less inviting than a lion's den; for Japanese officers were going in and out through the swing doors and two were actually talking on the steps. But Gimlet did not hesitate. Without giving Cub time to ponder on the peril of the undertaking he went straight on up the steps.

After a quick glance along the street to make sure

that Trapper could see what they were doing, Cub followed Gimlet into the hotel vestibule. He was relieved to see two tired-looking Frenchmen talking in a corner, for until then he had an uncomfortable feeling that the hotel might be barred to Europeans, excepting those on official business.

The only other person in the spacious hall was an Oriental youth, dressed Chinese fashion, who was watering some palms in big blue pots near the reception office. It struck Cub that he surveyed them with more interest than the occasion demanded; indeed, he looked at them for so long, and in such a covert manner, that the pot he was watering overflowed. However, it seemed that if Gimlet observed this interest he attached to it no particular significance, for he walked straight on towards the stairs with as much self-assurance as if he had been the proprietor, leaving Cub to follow. On the right the dining-room doors stood wide open, permitting a clear view of a considerable gathering of Japanese officers, both naval and military, to whom Chinese waiters were serving meals. Cub glanced into the room in passing. It all looked very unreal. He found it hard to believe that what he saw, and what he was doing, was actually happening. He overtook Gimlet half way up the stairs.

"I have an idea that Chinese boy down below is watching us," he warned.

This information Gimlet acknowledged with a barely perceptible nod. He neither stopped nor looked round, but crossing the landing at the head of the stairs in two strides he grasped the handle of the door that faced them, turned it and pushed the door open.

Cub held his breath, and then released it in something like a gasp of relief. There was no one in the room. Moreover, there was ample evidence that it was the room they sought, the reading-room, for a large central table was strewn with papers and magazines.

Gimlet closed the door behind them. "All nice and easy so far," he murmured.

"So far," echoed Cub, whose heart was thumping with some violence. He could not forget that the Japanese method of execution was decapitation, the thought of which never failed to give him a prickling sensation at the nape of the neck. Even so, his eyes flashed round the room, seeking the object which they were taking such risks to secure—the ebony elephant. He did not expect to see it. In his heart he felt sure that during the long interval of time it would have been taken away—stolen, lost, broken . . . all sorts of things could have happened to it. But no. There, in the end wall, was the niche; and in it, against a cream background almost as conspicuous as a live animal would have been, was the elephant, a black image about ten inches high, its trunk upraised.

"It's still here," he said in a voice of wonder. "Let's grab it and go."

"Take it easy," answered Gimlet with a calmness that was like ice-water on Cub's heated imagination. "We can't get away with a thing that size. Besides, we don't want it. Get the seeds."

Cub needed no second invitation. He sped across the room, reached up and took the elephant from its resting place. As he did so a chill seemed to freeze his enthusiasm, for he realized suddenly that if the seeds were still inside the image they would have rattled, or made some sound. Grasping the thing with both hands he shook it. Not a sound. With eyes wide with mortification he stared at Gimlet. "They've gone," he said through his teeth.

Gimlet walked over and joined him. He took the ornament and shook it with some violence. It might have been solid for all the response he got from inside. "I'm afraid you're right," he said evenly. "Pity."

Cub took the elephant again and blew down the hollow trunk with no result. With desperate energy he tore the corner off a newspaper, chewed it into a little round pellet and dropped it down the trunk. Then, tilting the ornament he poured it out again. "Empty," he said bitterly. "If the paper falls out so would the seeds. We must have been crazy to suppose that they could remain undiscovered all this time. The seeds probably fell out months ago when the thing was being dusted, in which case no doubt they would go into the dustbin."

Gimlet nodded. "Bad luck. I'm afraid our people will be disappointed, but there's nothing more we can do about it. We might as well go home."

Cub was nearly sick with disappointment, but it seemed the only thing to do. He had replaced the elephant and was turning away from the niche when a slight sound from the direction of the door brought him round with a start of alarm. Standing just inside the room was the Chinese boy he had remarked in the vestibule. Cub's pistol was out in a flash.

The boy raised a hand. "No use," said he, smoothly, speaking—to Cub's amazement and consternation— in English.

Cub was no longer concerned with such trivial things as seeds. They had gone, anyhow, so they could be dismissed from mind. At this critical juncture his one impulse was to get out of the place, and out of Saigon, with his head still on his shoulders; and it was with this object in view, still keeping the Chinese boy covered, that he advanced towards the door. "Don't move," he cautioned.

"No use," said the boy again. Then he added two words that brought Cub to a halt, blinking with incredulity. "Seeds gone," he said calmly. He still spoke in English.

Gimlet now stepped into the conversation. "What do you know about the seeds?" he asked crisply.

The boy did not answer the question. He looked from Gimlet to Cub and back to Gimlet. "You Blitish gentlemens?" he queried.

Gimlet hesitated, for once taken aback, by this unexpected question. "What makes you think we are British?"

"You no stay Saigon long time. Face white. No sun. Plenty sun Saigon."

Gimlet threw a sidelong glance at Cub. "He's right. We might have slipped up on that. We should have browned our faces." To the boy he said: "Yes, we are British."

The faintest suspicion of a smile crossed the boy's impassive face. "I wait long time for you to come. Watch elephant all time." He laid a finger on his lips. "No talkee here."

"Where can we talk?" asked Gimlet.

"Ting Loo opium house. Rue Lafayette, number ten. Soon I come."

"Are you sure Ting Loo is safe?" asked Cub anxiously.

"Say Chang Chu think plum blossom bloom again. Ting Loo fliend. Go now. General Onatishu eat in

A curious aroma hung in the air. Having shown them into the room the guide bowed again and retired, closing the door behind him.

dining room but bling coffee here soon." The boy bowed, opened the door, slipped through and was gone.

Gimlet also moved quickly. "Let's go," he said. "That boy knows something. We've got to take him on trust, but I think it's worth while if there's still a chance to get the seeds."

It seemed to Cub that this chance was so slim as to be unworthy of serious consideration. However, he said nothing, but opening the door looked down into the vestibule. He caught his breath. A Japanese officer, a senior officer judging by the amount of gold braid he wore, was coming up the stairs followed by a respectful retinue of staff officers.

Gimlet nudged Cub, and stepping out on to the landing stood still with bowed head. Cub took the cue and followed suit. The officers, with an exaggerated dignity that would have been comic on the stage, passed by with scarcely a glance. Only one looked at Cub—and he looked twice. He was a German captain. For a split second their eyes met, and Cub felt the blood drain from his face. He knew the man. It was the officer who, nearly two years before, had questioned him in the square at Chateaudun*. Here, thought Cub bitterly, was one of those capricious tricks of fate which no amount of planning could forestall. However, the German went on. As the retinue filed into the reading-room he threw yet another glance over his shoulder. His forehead was creased in a puzzled frown. Cub knew what was passing in his mind. The German knew that he had seen Cub before and was wondering where. It would worry him. Presently, in five minutes or five hours, he would remember. As the door closed

See "King" of the Commandos.

behind the Japanese general and his staff Cub moistened his lips.

Said Gimlet: "That must have been Onatishu and his staff."

"Let's get out," returned Cub tersely. "I've been spotted. That German knew me."

"Oh dear," murmured Gimlet. "Pity about that. Never mind, keep your head."

"That's just what I want to do," answered Cub.

They went on down the stairs. Japanese officers and an occasional civilian were still passing in and out through the swing doors. Gimlet, with Cub at his elbow, joined them, and went down the steps into the street. He walked on a little way before pulling up close to the front wall of the building.

"Surprising what one can do with a little nerve and plenty of cheek, isn't it?" he murmured, smiling faintly.

"Yes," answered Cub without enthusiasm. He told Gimlet of the occasion when the German had spoken to him. "Sooner or later he'll remember where he last saw me. He knew I was associated with you. He'll remember that, too."

Trapper was standing a little further along watching the hotel entrance with an air of bored indifference. Gimlet, by an inclination of his head, indicated that he was to follow them. To Cub he said: "The next business is to find the Rue Lafayette. Your French is better than mine so you'd better inquire."

Cub asked a native policeman who was standing at a corner swinging a baton, and having received the desired information he set off, leaving the others to follow.

IV

The Rue Lafayette turned out to be an insalubrious side-street, which suited Cub because it seemed to be little used by the men from whom they had most to fear—the Japanese. Number ten was a shop of sorts, a place of strange smells in which were offered for sale a nondescript collection of oddments, objects which in a European country would have been thrown on the scrapheap. It was tended by an Oriental of uncertain age and nationality, and to this man, with Gimlet and Trapper standing behind him, Cub addressed himself in French.

"We come from Chang Chu who says he thinks the plum blossom will bloom again," said Cub.

The expression on the face before him did not change. All the man did was bow low and lead the way through the shop along a corridor of some length which ended in a small extremely shabby room, lighted by a tiny oil lamp, with four wooden bunks fitted against the walls. The bunks were provided with blankets and pillows that had obviously seen better days. A curious aroma hung in the air. Having shown them into the room the guide bowed again and retired, closing the door behind him.

"Now what do we do?" asked Cub.

"Wait," answered Gimlet, seating himself on a bunk and lighting a cigarette. "Either that Chinese boy, Chang Chu, or whatever he called himself, will arrive, or, if he happens to be a spy, a squad of Jap soldiers. Personally, I'd bet on the boy. There was something about his manner that impressed me—struck

31

me as genuine. We're taking a chance by trusting him, but if we are to get what we came for there was no alternative. The seeds are no longer in the hotel, that's certain. Whether they are still in existence remains to be seen." He told Trapper what had happened at the hotel. "It's a pity about that German spotting Cub, but it was just one of those things," he concluded.

"We ought to be safe here," observed Trapper.

Cub looked round. "This, I imagine, is an opium den?"

Trapper nodded. "Sure. I once saw the inside of one in Vancouver."

"I hope that boy isn't going to be long," muttered Cub. "I feel uncomfortably like a rat in a trap."

Trapper grunted. "When you deal with Chinese the thing you want most is patience."

"We may as well take the opportunity to rest," put in Gimlet. "On a job like this it's good policy to rest when you can—but I don't think I shall need these disgusting bedclothes." He emptied the bunk of its contents and stretched himself at full length.

Cub did the same and settled down to wait. In spite of his conviction that he would not be able to sleep he must have dozed, for he opened his eyes with a start to see the Chinese boy standing there. Looking quickly at his watch he was astonished to see that it was six o'clock. The others were awake, so swinging his legs over the edge of the bunk he waited with interest to hear what the boy had to say.

Chang Chu's first words were not reassuring. "Bad, velly bad," he began.

"What's bad?" asked Gimlet.

"Japanese mens say spies in Saigon," answered

Chang. "Soldiers look everywhere; stand on roads."

Gimlet glanced at Cub. "It looks as if that German *attaché* has remembered when and where he saw you," he remarked drily. "No matter. Such chances are part of the game." He looked back at Chang. "Now, what about these seeds?" he prompted.

"You fliends Sir Radnor *sahib*?" queried the boy.

"We are," asserted Gimlet.

"You come for seeds?"

"Yes. How did you know that?"

"I wait. Wait long time. Watchee all people go to room with elephant." The boy sat down on the edge of a spare bunk and tucked his hands into his sleeves.

"Tell us what you know about the seeds," invited Gimlet.

"Charla Song honourable uncle of me," explained the boy. "I live with him long time. He teachee me spik English. He say wait, watch elephant. One day man come for seeds. I take work at hotel and watch."

"The seeds are no longer in the elephant," said Gimlet. "Do you know where they are?"

"Yes, I know."

"Where are they?"

"Japanese men take them away to Japan to make grow into trees," said the boy.

Cub was shocked, mortified. As they could not go to Japan this seemed like the end of the mission.

"Why didn't you say at once that the seeds were lost?" demanded Gimlet.

"Seeds go Japan no use," answered Chang blandly. "Japanese men not understand Chinese. Charla Song know Japanese will look for seeds, plaps find. So he change seeds. Seeds go Japan no use. Allee same other trees."

Cub thrilled. He began to see daylight. The genuine seeds might not be lost after all.

At Gimlet's request, the boy, in his quaint and sometimes laboured English, told his story. The conclusion was disappointing but not final. It all amounted to this.

Sir Lionel Radnor had been seized and taken to Japan where, on his refusal to divulge the hiding place of the seeds, he had been murdered. This of course was already known. A new factor was now introduced. Charla Song had evaded arrest, but like a faithful servant he hung about in the hope of keeping in touch with his employer. In this he had for a time succeeded. From a tree in the garden of the hotel he had spoken to Sir Lionel and in this way had learned of the hiding place of the seeds. Sir Lionel had asked him to send word to the British, and this he had done, by a Burmese. On Sir Lionel's arrest and removal from the hotel, Charla Song, with shrewd foresight, had realized that the Japanese would sooner or later learn of the seeds and make a search for them. The reading room would be one of the first places examined, and it was hardly likely that the elephant would be overlooked. This, in the event, was correct. But in the meantime Charla Song had entered the room and substituted twenty ordinary seeds for the special ones, which he had taken away with him to keep in safe custody until such time as they could be handed over to the British, feeling sure that the British government would try to recover them. He had made provision for this by getting a nephew, Chang Chu, to obtain employment at the hotel to watch for British agents whom he felt sure would come, if the Burmese got through with his message. So far all had gone as planned. But tragedy was to follow. Charla Song had bought a small house

34

on the outskirts of the town, and had he been able to remain in hiding he might still have been in it with the seeds in his possession. Unfortunately for him he had been seen and recognized by a man whom he had once discharged for petty theft. The man had betrayed him to the Japanese. Realizing what was likely to happen Charla Song had hidden the seeds so well that they could not be found. He had been seized, questioned under torture, and finally decapitated, without divulging where he had put the seeds.

At this juncture Gimlet interrupted the story. "If your uncle was killed how do you know about all this?" he asked.

Chang explained that he had listened to Japanese officers talking in the hotel. His information was, the Japanese had promised Charla Song that if he gave then the seeds they would not kill him. If he refused, they would chop his head off. "Japanese chop head off, so he no tell," concluded the boy with simple logic.

"But just a minute," put in Cub. "I can see a snag in this. You say the Japanese found the seeds in the elephant. If they had the seeds, or thought they had them, why should they question your uncle?"

Chang smiled sadly. "By this time they know the seeds they find no use. They fly seeds to Japan in aeroplane. Seeds grow quickly in special garden in Tokyo. Japanese rubber men say trees no use—same like any other rubber tree."

"I get it," murmured Gimlet. "We must remember that this business started more than two years ago. When the seeds germinated the Japs would soon spot that they were the common or garden variety." To Chang he went on. "How long is it since your uncle was killed?"

Chang said it was just over a year.

"And so you don't know what became of the special seeds?" questioned Gimlet.

The boy answered no.

"Have you looked for them?"

"Yes, many times."

"Then it seems pretty hopeless," muttered Cub. "If Chang can't find them what hope have we got?"

"Does anyone live in your uncle's house now?" Gimlet asked Chang.

"No," answered the boy again. He went on to explain that in their search for the seeds the Japanese had nearly pulled the house to pieces.

"*Tch!* It gets worse and worse," remarked Trapper pessimistically. "I guess we might as well go home."

"I'm not so sure of that," returned Gimlet. "We know from the way he behaved right through this affair that Charla Song was no fool. Far from it. He knew the Japs would look for those seeds, so when he hid them we may be sure it would be no ordinary hiding place—otherwise the Japs would find them. The Japs didn't find them, so the chances are they are still where he put them. Whether we can find them is another matter."

"If the Japs couldn't I reckon we shan't," opined Trapper.

Chang Chu made it clear that his uncle had no opportunity to tell him where he had hidden the seeds. Charla was thrown straight into prison where it was impossible to get in touch with him.

"But your uncle must have known that was likely to happen," averred Cub. "What would he do in the circumstances? He had brains and he knew how to use them. I'd say that failing to get in touch with you he would leave a clue of some sort to the whereabouts of the seeds."

"*Ma foi!* But if he left the clue that Chang could read the Japs would be able to read it," declared Trapper.

"Not necessarily," argued Cub. "He wouldn't be such a fool as to leave a clue like that. It would be something essentially Chinese, something that only a Chinese would understand."

"But Chang didn't find a clue or he would have followed it up," Trapper pointed out.

"Maybe, but there is something in Cub's line of argument," put in Gimlet thoughtfully. "The least we can do now we are here is make a search of Charla's house, if Chang will tell us where it is."

Chang not only expressed his willingness to do this, but offered to take them. In describing the direction and position of the house to them it was revealed that the place was on the side of Saigon from which they had entered the town, some three miles nearer to Copper and the dump than they were at the moment —which, as Trapper remarked, was one bit of luck, anyway. This however was balanced by difficulties. Chang could not go immediately as he was supposed to be on duty at the hotel, and would be until midnight; which meant that he would not be free to act as guide until that time. He pointed out that this did not really matter, though, as they would not be able to do much searching in the dark. They would have to wait for dawn to see what they were doing. He, Chang, might stay with them for a little while, but he would have to be back on duty at the hotel by six o'clock the next morning. He assured them that they were quite safe where they were, much safer than outside. He would ask Ting Loo to bring them tea.

As nothing more could be done at the moment, Chang then departed and the others settled down again to kill time pending his return.

v

It was twenty minutes past midnight when Chang opened the door and announced himself with one of his courteous bows. He had no fresh news beyond the fact that the search for the British spies was being conducted with energy and thoroughness. Not only were the roads being watched but the populace had been warned that to provide strangers with food and lodging would be punished by instant death—a threat which, said Chang with a ghost of a smile, would have no effect on the Chinese. He suggested that they should proceed to his uncle's house without loss of time. As far as possible he would keep to the native quarter of the town. He said he would go first. The others were to follow him.

Ting Loo, still in his little shop, said not a word, but bowed low as they filed out into the street.

Night had fallen. The moon had not yet risen, but a wealth of stars made the street lighter than Cub would have wished. There was no street lighting. The only artificial light was an occasional glimmer from badly-fitting doors and windows. Chang strode on ahead. The others followed in single file with Trapper bringing up the rear.

In this order the party proceeded for some distance with Chang obviously avoiding main roads, for the way lay through such a labyrinth of dark narrow streets that Cub began seriously to wonder how they would find their way out should anything happen to their guide. At last, however, it became necessary to cross a main road, for, as Chang explained, the objective lay on the far side of it, so the crossing would have to be made sooner or later. As the street appeared there was no immediate cause for alarm; not a soul was in sight, as Chang ascertained by a quick reconnaissance. He seemed to be nervous, though, that unseen eyes might be watching. And in this, as it turned out, he was right. Standing in deep shadow Gimlet decided that they should cross the road one at a time. He would go first. If nothing happened the others were to follow. But hardly had he stepped from the black background of the house against which he had been standing than another figure detached itself from the wall and advanced towards him. The starlight gleamed dully on a fixed bayonet, and Cub's nerves twitched as he recognized a Japanese soldier. The meeting of Gimlet and the soldier took place in the street less than ten yards from where the others crouched; or, it would be more correct to say, the Jap intercepted Gimlet, and uttered what was clearly a challenge. Gimlet stopped, as he was bound to, and in a flash the point of the bayonet was threatening him, within six inches of his chest.

Cub held his breath. He felt Trapper move against his right arm. Out of the corners of his eyes he saw him straighten himself, although with what object he did not know. By this time the Jap was speaking loudly and harshly to his prisoner, and with the point of his bayonet forced him to turn. The mere fact that his prisoner was a white man seemed sufficient excuse for using his bayonet on him. Burning with resentment Cub whipped out his pistol, but before he could use it Gimlet himself had acted. He spun round, sidestepping

39

like a cat as he did so, at the same time grasping the menacing bayonet; but in doing this he slipped on the greasy road and fell. The Jap tore his bayonet clear and in a flash it was raised to strike. Trapper's right arm went up and his body jerked like a steel spring. There was a vicious thud. The Jap gasped. His rifle fell with a noisy clatter on the road as with both hands he clutched at his breast. Then his legs crumpled under him and he dropped. Gimlet scrambled to his feet.

In the shadow Trapper took charge. "Over you go," he told Cub tersely, and without waiting for him he ran into the road. What he said to Gimlet Cub did not hear, but after a quick glance up and down the road Gimlet went on to the far side, when Cub and Chang joined them. Telling the others to follow Chang ran a little way before halting in another shadow to look back.

Presently Trapper joined them. "Okay, sir," he said calmly.

"Thanks," returned Gimlet. "Nice work."

"It's a nice knife," said Trapper simply.

"What did you do with him?"

"Dumped him in a garden where I hope he won't be found until morning."

"Good. It was him or me for it, and at one moment I thought it was going to be me. Let's get along. Lead on, Chang."

Chang went on, walking more quickly now. What he thought of the incident, if he thought about it at all, was not revealed.

A walk of a quarter of an hour brought the party to the outskirts of the town. Houses began to give way to market gardens and cultivated fields, then to

40

areas of dense jungle with only an occasional dwelling of native type here and there, holding its own, it seemed, with difficulty against the ever encroaching forest. Chang took a turning to the right, up a track half overgrown. After going on a little way he stopped and pointed to a small bungalow some twenty yards beyond an area of weeds that occupied what had once evidently been a garden.

"The house of my honourable uncle," he said simply.

"Thank you, Chang," answered Gimlet. "We shan't be able to do much to-night, but we'll do what we can when it starts to get light. You needn't stay if you'd rather go. In case we don't see you again please accept our thanks for what you have done; I'll see that it is brought to the notice of the British government. Perhaps before you go you had better show us the best way into the house."

Chang replied by forcing a passage through a thin part of the undergrowth, along what had once been a path, to the house. The door stood ajar, hanging on a single hinge. They went in. The beam of Gimlet's torch sliced a wedge of light in the darkness to probe the extremities of the little room in which they found themselves. There was nothing but bare walls. Not a stick of furniture remained.

Cub said nothing, but it seemed to him that to start searching such a place for an object as small as a packet of seeds was a sheer waste of time.

"I suppose you searched the house thoroughly for writing of any sort?" said Gimlet to Chang.

"I find no writing," answered the boy.

"What's this?" inquired Trapper, stooping to pick up a flimsy oblong-shaped piece of paper that lay half buried in debris on the floor. It was damp, dirty and torn, but had been more or less held together by slithers of bamboo at the top and bottom.

"It is picture writing, a saying of Tao, for a text of the house," explained Chang. "It was on wall. Japs tear down, or plaps wind blow down."

In the reflected light of the torch Trapper looked at the brush-written Chinese characters on the paper. "What does it say?" he asked.

Chang answered quietly "By still water in a garden is happiness found."

"*Tch!* Maybe Tao had something there," murmured Trapper, dropping the paper.

Gimlet switched off the light. "All right, Chang. You had better get back. Good-bye and good luck."

"The honour is for me," said Chang. He bowed, and a minute later could be heard pushing his way through the weeds towards the track.

"I'm afraid this is where we have another spell of waiting," said Gimlet softly. "We'll spend to-morrow searching. When it gets dark we'll push along back to Copper. I hope he's all right. He ought to be warned that things are humming, but with the roads being watched I doubt if the risk of trying to get in touch with him is worth while. Trapper, will you take the first watch?"

"Sure, sir," answered Trapper.

VI

Dawn brought evidence that the hunt for strangers in Saigon was still going on. Low-flying aircraft bearing the Rising Sun insignia of Japan raced overhead, and twice during the morning the systematic search that was being made in Charla Song's bungalow was held up while small but busy patrols of Japanese troops marched past down the track.

To Cub the search was never more than a matter of routine, something that had to be done without any real hope of success. Not normally pessimistic, in this case he felt that to look for an object as small as a packet of seeds, in a building that had already been half pulled to pieces by others actuated by the same motive, was futile. Trapper's expression suggested that he felt the same way about it; always taciturn, he assisted in the business with thoroughness but without enthusiasm. However, Gimlet persevered, observing that as they were there, and would have to remain there until nightfall, they might as well employ their time usefully.

"Those seeds are here if only we could find them," he asserted more than once. "Charla Song wouldn't hide them anywhere else, and as the Japs didn't find them they *must* be here."

"Knowing what was likely to happen to him I must say it seemed mad to hide them so well that no one could find them, not even Chang," argued Cub. "Moreover, he seems to have assumed that British agents would come out to look for them. Sooner or later they would come to this house—yet what use would that be if the seeds were so well hidden that it was impossible to find them?"

"He had to hide them where the Japs couldn't find them," returned Gimlet. "It may be that he left a clue which the Japs in their desperate search have destroyed."

"The place is damp," stated Trapper moodily. "The rain must have poured in during the monsoon. Damp and heat would make the seeds grow."

43

"They were in a tin," reminded Gimlet.

"If it was airtight they'd go mouldy," said Trapper. "I once tried to bring home seeds of a special Douglas fir for the afforestation people, but they all went rotten on me. I carried them in an old tobacco tin."

"Charla Song, being Sir Lionel's assistant, would know the risk of that," remarked Cub.

Towards evening Cub went out into the overgrown garden. To search the ground under the rank weeds, which covered the best part of an acre, without tools to clear the tangle, was obviously impossible. He forced a way to the end where, under a weeping willow, he found a small artificial pool. Beside it was a crumbling wooden bench. He sat precariously on it and gazed at the water. Its placid surface reminded him of the text of the house. "By still water in a garden is happiness found," he mused. Here, he realized, Charla Song must have sat many times in earnest contemplation, seeking happiness. For the first time it struck him that there might be a hidden message in the text. Could the seeds be at the bottom of the pool, in a watertight container? It was an idea. The area round the pool was certainly less overgrown than the rest, as if it had once been kept in good order, under careful cultivation. There were still flowers, and small flowering shrubs.

Kneeling, Cub explored the water with his hands. As it was shallow there was no difficulty in this; but all he found was rotting leaves, slime, and a dead goldfish. Rinsing his hands he returned to the bench. "By still water . . . is happiness found," he murmured. Here certainly was still water—but to what particular happiness, if any, did Charla refer?

Cub's eyes lifted from the pool and began a perfunctory survey of its immediate surroundings for a possible hiding place. Surely, he thought, Charla would not bury the seeds, for if he did they would grow. Yes, they would grow, thought Cub. A new angle suddenly struck him. Suppose they did grow—would it matter? Of course it wouldn't matter. His brain began to race. The young plants would have the same value as the seeds. In fact, they would be a year nearer to maturity. Seeds planted in the earth would defy the efforts of the entire Japanese army to find them—until they began to grow, anyway. His heart was beating fast now as the idea gathered impetus, and he saw ever more clearly that no more effective method of hiding the seeds could be devised. There would be no risk of mildew. The plants would live for years—and bear more seeds that would go on perpetuating themselves indefinitely.

He began to explore the area round the pool more closely. One place attracted his attention almost at once by virtue of the fact that it had been cultivated at a later date than anywhere else. It was marked off by small pieces of rock. In the marked area there were weeds, of course, but only soft weeds; there were no briars, or other woody growths. Kneeling, flattening the weeds gently with his hands, he found a seedling. It was stiff, about six inches high, carrying four tough dark-green leaves. Was it a young rubber tree? He did not know. He had never seen a young rubber tree. Searching on he found another, another, and another, in a straight line. He was weeding desperately now, tearing the weeds out with his hands to expose more and more seedlings, in neat lines. His common sense told him that these had been planted with deliberate care, for had they dropped haphazard they could hardly have fallen in rows as straight as if they had been ruled. When, in a few minutes, he had uncovered twenty seedlings, neither more nor less, in four rows of five, he felt certain that he was right. "Twenty," he breathed. He was *sure* he was right. There must be a limit to coincidence. Disregarding briars and trailing weeds that clutched at his legs he hurried back to the house, to find Gimlet and Trapper sitting on the floor, smoking, dejected, having abandoned the search.

"I've got 'em," he announced triumphantly. "At least, I think so," he added with a burst of caution.

Gimlet sprang to his feet. *"What?"*

"Come with me," invited Cub, and led the way to the miniature plantation. "Look!" he exclaimed, pointing at the seedlings. "Twenty! By still water in a garden is happiness found. Charla was too smart for the Japs. He *planted* the seeds."

Gimlet drew a deep breath. "By gad! You're right. Pretty work, Cub."

Trapper clicked his tongue. *"Mot de Cambronne!* What a trick. Charla must be laughing in his grave."

"The question is, how do we get them home?" muttered Gimlet. "If we dig them up they will die."

"Mais non," answered Trapper. "Not if we wrap the roots in damp moss and keep it damp. That is how it is done by the forestry men in Canada."

"Let's get busy," ordered Gimlet. "There's plenty of moss under the trees. We'll make three bundles and carry one each in case of accidents."

"What are we going to use to dig them up?" asked Cub.

"I'll get them up with my knife—you get the moss," answered Trapper, and set to work.

46

By the time the seedlings had been lifted, and, with some earth clinging to the fibrous roots, rolled into compact bundles of moss, it was nearly dark. Cub straightened his back, and was wiping sweat from his forehead when a crashing in the bushes near the house brought them all round facing that way.

"*Sahib! Sahib*" came a voice, brittle with urgency.

"It's Chang," said Gimlet tersely. "Something's happened. Bring the plants." He walked quickly towards the house.

Chang came to meet them. For the first time his oriental calm had broken down. He was hot, dishevelled, and breathing heavily, as if he had run a long way. "Go," he panted, as soon as he saw them. "Go quick. Japanese come."

"You mean they're coming here?" asked Gimlet.

"Yes, come here. Onatishu give orders Charla's house be watched for spies to come. I hear officers talk in hotel."

"Thanks, Chang," acknowledged Gimlet. "We've got what we came for so we'll clear out while we can. But what about you? If you were seen coming this way you may be suspect——" Gimlet broke off, listening. A vehicle—it sounded like a car—was coming up the track.

"Japanese," said Chang in a resigned voice.

"We'll soon see. Let's get in here." Gimlet forced a way into a thick group of shrubs. The others followed. "Quiet now," he ordered, for the car had stopped on the track in line with the bungalow. A voice spoke sharply, harshly, and a minute later weeds were being crushed and forced aside by advancing feet. In the fast-failing light a Japanese officer appeared, pistol in hand. He made straight for the house followed

47

by three soldiers carrying rifles. Reaching the door he went in, but very soon reappeared, and began giving orders to his men. From his actions he appeared to be allocating positions in the garden commanding a view of the door. Cub looked at Gimlet's face for a guide as to what he was thinking, for it was clear that they would not be able to move without being discovered. It was also clear that the party had come to stay, to watch the house. Trapper also looked at Gimlet questioningly, and with some concern. Chang, who had recovered his composure, stood impassive, presumably content to leave decisions to the white men.

How the matter would have ended had it not been for the introduction of a new factor into the drama is a matter for conjecture. It was quite a minor factor but, as so often happens in the conduct of human affairs, it played a major part. A slight movement near Cub's face caused him to switch his eyes in that direction, to observe, with loathing and horror, a centipede about six inches long. The bloated, many-legged creature, the shape and colour of an uncooked sausage, was moving with rippling undulations of its body along a dead branch that would presently bring it to within a few inches of Cub's face. This, he decided instantly, was too close. Whether the insect was poisonous or not did not arise. The movement that he made was involuntary. He stepped aside. His foot came down on another dead branch and as he shifted his weight the branch snapped with a crack. He moved again instantly, but the damage had been done. The Japanese officer broke off what he was saying. All four stared in the direction of the sound.

The enemy officer evidently saw them for his pistol

swung up. But Gimlet fired first. As he fired he said loudly: "Let 'em have it!"

After that things happened quickly. The Japanese officer fell back against the wall and slid to the ground. Gimlet fired again, and by this time Trapper and Cub were in action. The advantage of surprise was on their side and at such close range the enemy troops had little chance. In fact, they did not fire a shot. One dived for the door of the bungalow but fell before reaching it. The other two had already dropped. Gimlet watched for a moment or two, braced, alert, to make sure that none of them was able to lift a rifle. Then he said sharply: "Cub, get their caps."

"Caps?" queried Cub, not sure that he had understood the order.

"Caps I said," snapped Gimlet. "The noise of this shooting should start a first class flap. We'll get out, and we may as well ride. The caps may help to see us through."

Cub ran forward and brought back the four field-service caps. Gimlet tossed his panama into the bushes and put the officer's cap on his head. "Come on," he ordered, and strode towards the track. The car, an open Fiat, was there, unattended.

"This is going to be quicker than walking," said Gimlet, as he climbed into the driving seat. "Chang, sit beside me in case I need a guide. Cub, Trapper, get in behind and keep your guns handy. I'm not stopping for anything or anybody."

The engine started. Gimlet turned the car and cruised down the track, peering forward to see into the deceptive gloom that follows twilight and precedes the full darkness of night.

VII

Cub was not in the least surprised at Gimlet's decision to use the car. It was not the first time he had done that sort of thing—as much, Cub was sure, for the sheer devilment of it as for expediency. No doubt he would do it again, and it seemed not unlikely, mused Cub, as they cruised on down the track, that he would do it once too often. One of Gimlet's principles was, paradoxically, that the dangerous way was usually the safest, his argument being that the enemy would perceive the safe method and make the obvious counter-move. In the present case, thought Cub, Gimlet would no doubt argue that the enemy would not expect spies to be travelling in one of their own service cars. They would expect them to be creeping furtively round dark corners. And while there was something to be said for this it did not lessen the tension of employing the dangerous way. Wherefore Cub's nerves were strung tight as they ran out of the track into the main road, and turned to the right in the direction of the rendezvous. In such circumstances most men would tread on the accelerator with the object of getting out of the danger zone in the shortest possible space of time. But not Gimlet. Cub, from experience, was well aware of that. Gimlet cruised quietly along at a comfortable twenty miles an hour as if he might have been in London, on the way to his club.

For a while Gimlet's contention, that this was the safest as well as the easiest way of travelling, held good. There was a fair amount of traffic on the road including

50

naval and military transport, but no one took the slightest notice of the Fiat. Not that there was any reason why they should, for the car was identical with others, driven by genuine Japanese personnel. The first hitch came after the traffic had thinned, where the houses were beginning to be more widely spaced on the outskirts of the town. There was a four-cross-ways. Cub remembered the spot, for they had made a detour to bypass it when they had walked in. A soldier stood in the road on point duty. Two others stepped out as the car appeared. One held a note-book. The other raised a hand in a signal to stop. He did this quite casually, as if conscious of his authority. He had probably been doing it all day and his signal had always been obeyed. From the confident way he stood in the path of the advancing car it might never have occurred to him that a car would not stop at his command. This error of judgment was speedily corrected. The Fiat's siren howled a warning. The car leapt forward and the two soldiers escaped death by inches. What happened to them Cub never knew, for the car raced on.

"I'm afraid that will stir things up, but there was no other way." Gimlet threw the words back over his shoulder.

Four miles on, now with forest on both sides, there was a more serious obstruction. It was a barrier; but it was evidently more for effect than utility, for the middle of it had been left open so that cars could pass through one at a time. A convoy of lorries had been halted at the far side, and it was to the drivers of these vehicles that those on duty at the barrier were talking. Cub did not think they could get through, but Gimlet thought otherwise. He shot through the opening, spun the wheel, gave it another twist and went on along the line of lorries. There were shouts at this flagrant breach of regulations. A shot was fired, but by that time the car had reached the end lorry and Gimlet put the Fiat under cover by turning it behind it. He laughed as they sped on.

"*Ma foi!* That was a pretty piece of driving," Trapper told Cub seriously.

Cub did not comment. He had screwed his body to look back. "There's a car of some sort coming behind us," he said. "I can't see what it is; it's too dark under these trees; but it may be following us. It's travelling fast." He passed the information on to Gimlet.

"Pity about that," answered Gimlet. "We're nearly there. I was looking for a place to park the car. Never mind—I have a better idea. Take care of the plants, and when I say jump, jump out and go on down the road. That goes for you too, Chang. Keep close to the verge. Ready?"

"Okay, sir," answered Trapper.

Gimlet jammed on the brakes. As the car dry-skidded he called: "Jump!"

They all jumped, and, as ordered, ran on a little way. The lights of the Fiat went out. In two quick spins of the wheel Gimlet had turned the car across the crown of the road so that there was not enough room either side for a vehicle to pass. Leaving the car there he overtook the others, who paused to wait for him.

The oncoming car drew near, travelling at high speed. Its brakes screeched as its headlamps revealed the obstruction, but it was going too fast to avoid

52

collision. There were shouts of dismay, followed a split second later by a splintering crash.

"We'll leave them to sort it out," said Gimlet calmly, and went on down the road, keeping well into the side.

Apart from an occasional halt in the fringe of the forest while a car passed, travelling towards Saigon, there was no further incident; and in a trifle over half an hour they had joined Copper at the dump. He had nothing to report, except that there had been a good deal of traffic on the road. He seemed far more concerned with the mosquitos that had made waiting a misery. Gimlet announced that they would eat before going on.

"Blimy, sir. I thought you was never comin'," grumbled Copper, ripping the lid off a can of bully beef. "Did yer get the seeds?"

Gimlet stated briefly what had happened. Then he looked at his watch. "We've got seven hours before the aircraft is due," he told them. "We ought to allow two hours to get to the boat, half an hour for launching, and two hours for paddling out to the rendezvous—we shall be going against the current, remember. But we may be delayed, so as soon as we've had something to eat we'll push along. What are you going to do, Chang? I don't think Saigon is going to be a safe place for you after this. Why not come with us—as far as India, anyway? I can get you a job there."

It did not take Chang long to make up his mind. He said he would go with them.

Half an hour later the march to the boat was begun, and at twelve midnight they reached it without having been seriously delayed or otherwise inconvenienced. Not that they had the road to themselves. Car patrols, motor cycles, and troops on bicycles, often passed, travelling one way or the other, making it evident that the hunt was still going strong; but the forest was always at hand for cover, so, as Copper remarked, "There was nothing to get in a sweat about." But when, carrying the dinghy, they arrived at the beach, where the trees ended and the sand began, things took a more serious turn. An aircraft, flying very low, cruised along the beach, with a broad beam of light directed downwards from a powerful lamp fitted under the nacelle.

"Hm. They know it isn't much good looking for us in the jungle, so they're patrolling the beach," observed Gimlet.

A minute later the vibrant throb of a fast motor-boat passed by, about half a mile out to sea.

"They're giving the briny the once-over, too," remarked Copper.

"If these patrols are working to a time-table, on regular beats, we ought to be able to dodge them," averred Gimlet. "Let's wait and see. We've a little time in hand."

They waited for fifty minutes—that is, until one o'clock. In that time the aircraft flew past once, and the motor-boat went past twice. The motor-boat was then coming back for the third time. Five minutes later the aircraft roared overhead.

The moment it had passed Gimlet said: "This is our chance. If they stick to their routine we ought to have the best part of half an hour to get clear."

The dinghy was rushed down to the sea and launched.

"Now," said Gimlet crisply. "Put your backs into it."

54

The clumsy craft surged forward through the placid water.

VIII

The dinghy was nearly a mile from shore, moving sluggishly against the current when, half an hour later, the aircraft raced low along the beach, its lamp revealing its position clearly. Gimlet remarked that they had little to fear from it now, unless the pilot changed his tactics and turned in a seaward direction. This is precisely what he did, and Cub held his breath as the machine came roaring back, just above the water and almost in line with them. Before reaching them however, the pilot swung back towards the shore to take up his regular beat, with the result that the radius of light flashed past about fifty yards distant.

"Why don't 'e stick to 'is beat?" growled Copper. "This messin' about is enough ter make a man swallow 'is tonsils."

"Don't talk so much, corporal," chided Gimlet. "Paddle."

"Aye—aye, sir."

Hardly had the drone of the aircraft died away than the throb of the motor-boat could be heard returning, and Cub perceived that everything now depended on whether the boat had turned seaward or towards the land at the end of its run. There was no moon, but the stars were bright, so that visibility was about half a mile. The dinghy had this advantage; it was low in the water, so that at a distance of anything over a quarter of a mile it stood a good chance of being overlooked.

They all crouched low as the speedy craft churned

up the water not more than five hundred yards away. Again it was a nasty moment, but the motor-boat raced on and Cub breathed again.

"Are there any sharks in this sea, sir?" asked Copper anxiously.

"Plenty, and if you go on talking we're all likely to make their acquaintance," returned Gimlet. "Paddle."

The dinghy ploughed on through the sullen water. There was nothing now to show how much progress was being made, for the shore-line was an unchanging silhouette. One thing that worried Cub was how they were going to make a signal to their aircraft without the light being seen by the patrols; for in the darkness through which they moved he felt that the merest spark would shine like a beacon. However, he said nothing, but continued dipping his paddle with perspiration pouring down his face, for the humid air was hot and sticky. He had this comfort though; every stroke was taking them farther from the shore, and the farther they got from the shore the less was the likelihood of their being discovered. The thrust and swish of paddles became an automatic movement. Gradually, very gradually, the silhouette of the shore became fainter. The light of the patrolling aircraft flashed along it, but it now seemed far away. Gimlet told them that the time was two-thirty.

"Bigglesworth will be here in half an hour," he asserted.

"If nothing comes unstuck," murmured Copper in a low voice.

"He'll be here," declared Gimlet. "He said he would be, so he will be."

56

"Let's hope you're right," breathed Copper. "If my old Ma could see me now——"

"She'd tell you to stop grousing and get on with the job," put in Gimlet.

"That's just about what she would say," agreed Copper sadly.

The next half hour seemed to Cub like an entire night. The time passed with exasperating slowness. Twice Gimlet ordered them to rest their paddles while he listened, face turned to the stars.

"Five minutes to go," he announced at last. "We should soon be hearing the machine."

All Cub could hear was the throb of the returning motor-boat; it was some distance away, but close enough to cause anxiety.

Again Gimlet spoke. "All right—rest," he ordered.

Silence fell. The only sounds were the hum of the patrol boat and the gentle lap of water against the sides of the dinghy. All around, as far as the eye could see, was the black expanse of ocean, a world of utter loneliness, immutable, far removed, it seemed, from the affairs of men.

Then, from far away, high in the western sky, came a sound like the sighing of wind in trees.

"That's 'im," muttered Copper.

"He's gliding down from the ceiling with his engines off," said Gimlet. "Make a shield with your jackets while I show the light."

In silence, with everyone aware that this was the critical moment, the signal was flashed. There was a pause, all eyes staring upward trying to probe the darkness.

Then Copper moved uneasily, turning his face towards the sound of the motor-boat, which seemed to be coming nearer. "I don't want nobody ter think I'm windy, but that boat ain't as far away as it was," he stated.

"I think you're right," agreed Gimlet. "No matter. Bigglesworth must have seen our light. We shall have to show it again in a minute. He told me on the way out that in jobs like this the snag is the risk of collision with the boat on the water through trying to land too close to it. Listen!"

"*Tch!* He's getting closer," said Trapper, staring up.

"So's that perishing motor-boat," muttered Copper.

This was obviously true, but nothing could be done about it. Cub strained his eyes upward, conscious that the next few minutes would settle the matter. It was a little while—perhaps two minutes although it seemed longer—before he saw the aircraft; then, suddenly, it was there, a monstrous winged creature low over the water coming straight towards them.

Gimlet flashed the light. "Stand by," he ordered.

With a long-drawn swish the keel of the flying boat cut a glowing scar in the smooth face of the water. The aircraft slowed and settled down amid dancing wavelets about a hundred yards from the dinghy.

"By Jove! That was pretty to watch," said Gimlet. He looked round suddenly as the hum of the patrolling motor-boat increased in volume. "Paddle!" he cried. "They've seen us!"

Those in the dinghy needed no urging, for the danger was apparent. Whether the crew of the motor-boat had seen the aircraft, or the glow of its exhausts, or Gimlet's signal light, was never known; but the bows of the racing craft were now turned seaward.

It was perhaps a quarter of a mile away. The dinghy had only fifty yards to go, but its speed, compared with that of the motor-boat, was negligible.

A figure appeared at the open cabin door of the aircraft. A voice shouted: "Step on it!" A machine gun in the bows of the motor-boat started its vicious chatter, to be answered at once from two turrets of the Catalina. Tracer cut lines of fire through the intervening darkness.

Cub was in no position to watch events, for the dinghy was now almost alongside the aircraft. Dropping his paddle he took the painter in his hand and made a grab at the cabin door. He missed it and would have gone overboard had not a hand reached out and dragged him into the machine. There was a moment of confusion, for the noise was now considerable—a medley of roaring engines and snarling machine guns. Someone shouted in a voice shrill with urgency.

Turning inside the machine to look out Cub saw a fearful sight. The motor-boat was in flames. That did not upset him, but the course it was taking did. It was rushing straight towards the Catalina as if the crew, knowing they were lost, were determined that those in the aircraft should share their fate. The Catalina's engines bellowed. The big aircraft began to move, slowly at first but swiftly gathering speed. For a few seconds it was touch and go; then the motor-boat, streaming flame and leaving a wake of burning oil, shot past the flying boat's rudder so close that the tail-unit rocked in the turbulent water of its track. But the danger was over. For a hundred yards or so the motor-boat continued its meteoric career; then, in a blinding sheet of flame, it blew up, scattering burning debris far and wide. Cub fell back into a seat.

The ginger-haired officer fastened the cabin door and turned a smiling face. "What you might call ending up with a bang," he observed cheerfully.

"There's an enemy aircraft in the offing; if the pilot sees the blaze we're all likely to end up with a bang," answered Cub.

"Is there, by jingo?" returned the officer, becoming serious. He hurried forward and disappeared. At the same time vibration ceased as the Catalina became airborne.

Cub drew a deep breath of relief, and looking round saw that the others were there. "Well, we made it," he remarked, for something to say.

"By the skin of our teeth," answered Copper. "If my 'air ain't white in the morning it won't be the fault of that flaming motor-boat."

"I'll take care of the seedlings now," said Gimlet. He collected the little bundles. "You fellows can settle down to rest. The fun's over."

"Fun," whispered Copper brokenly. "He calls it fun."

"What was that, corporal?" inquired Gimlet.

"Nothing, sir."

"Talking to yourself again?"

"Yessir."

Squadron Leader Bigglesworth appeared from the forward bulkhead door. "My partner, Algy Lacey, has taken over the stick; he knows the way home," he told Gimlet. "Glad you got back all right," he continued casually. "How did you get on?"

"Oh, so-so, you know," answered Gimlet.

"Get what you went for?"

"More or less."

"Have any trouble?" asked the pilot.

"Nothing to make a song about," returned Gimlet.

The squadron leader nodded. "Good. Well, we'll soon have you home," he promised, and went back to the cockpit.

Copper nudged Cub. "Nothing ter make a song about," he breathed. "Well, chum, I only 'ope I ain't with 'im when he starts singin'. What say you, Trapper? Am I right?"

Trapper grunted. "Every time, pal," he agreed warmly.

Cub smiled, yawned, and settled down in his seat.

STORY

2

ON THE HOME FRONT

A "Worrals" Of The W.A.A.F. Story

SQUADRON OFFICER JOAN WORRAL-SON, known to her intimate friends as "Worrals," walked briskly along the cinder track to the headquarters buildings of No. 21 Balloon Wing. "This looks like it," she remarked to her companion, Flight Officer Betty Lovell, more often called "Frecks." She stopped, rapped on a door, entered and saluted the flight-lieutenant who sat at the adjutant's desk.

"I'm Squadron Officer Worralson," she reported. "I'm here on the instructions of Air Commodore Raymond, of the Intelligence branch. He has sent me to investigate the complaint of an aircraftwoman named Norma Day."

The adjutant got up. His manner was one of slightly bored toleration. "The C.O.'s expecting you," he stated. "The Air Ministry rang up. We've got the girl here, too, to save time. Just a minute." He opened an inner door, spoke to someone in the next room and looked back over his shoulder. "Come in," he invited.

As Worrals and Frecks went through an officer

wearing the badges of rank of a wing commander rose to meet them. They shook hands.

"You know why I've come down, sir?" said Worrals.

"Yes, you've come to talk to that girl who's got a bee in her bonnet."

A little frown creased Worral's forehead. "I've been sent to interview Aircraftwoman Day," she replied a trifle stiffly. "I'll form my own opinion about this alleged bee in a bonnet when I've heard what she has to say."

The C.O. shrugged. "You're not proposing to question the verdict of a coroner's jury, I imagine?" said he, drily.

"I most certainly shall, if I find grounds to warrant it," returned Worrals calmly.

"It is my opinion that this girl's friend, Doris Marchant, drowned herself, and apparently the coroner thought so too, since he returned a verdict of 'found drowned,' " replied the wing commander.

"I'll reserve my opinion until I've spoken to Aircraftwoman Day," answered Worrals evenly. "I'm told she's here."

"I'll have her brought in." The C.O. touched a bell.

"I'd rather talk to her alone if you don't mind, sir," requested Worrals.

The wing commander smiled wearily. "Going to turn me out of my own office, eh?"

"Not at all, sir—if you can find other accommodation for us," said Worrals. "I prefer to see the girl alone. She may speak with more confidence if there isn't a man present."

The C.O' nodded. "I see. How long are you likely to be?"

"I shall be as quick as I can, sir," returned Worrals. "I flew down. My machine is parked at East Weald and I'd like to get back to base before dark."

The C.O. went out, to return presently with a slim, dark-eyed girl in W.A.A.F. uniform. "This is Aircraftwoman Day," he said as the girl saluted. "I'll leave you to it."

"Thanks, sir."

Worrals waited until the door was closed, then pulled out a chair. "Sit down, Norma," she said quietly. "Your report on the death of Doris Marchant was forwarded to the Higher Command, so I've come down to have a chat with you about it. I've read your report, but I'd like you to tell the story in your own words—what you really think, how you feel about it, and why. Get the whole thing off your chest, so to speak." Worrals spoke with her eyes on the girl's face. She noted that it was pale. Dark rings round the eyes spoke eloquently of recent tears.

Norma sat down. "They're trying to make out that Doris drowned herself," she said in a hard bitter voice. "It's a lie. I know it's a lie. She was murdered. She was——" The girl broke off, biting her lip. Her eyes filled with tears.

"All right, take it easy," put in Worrals gently. "We shan't get anywhere, you know, if you're going to get all worked up. What makes you think Doris Marchant was murdered?"

"She was my friend, and has been for years," went on Norma brokenly. "We told each other

65

everything. She had no reason to kill herself, and as she could swim she couldn't have been drowned by accident in a river the size of the Ouse."

"Are these the only reasons that make you think she was murdered?" asked Worrals.

"No. There were other things, but nobody will believe me when I tell them about it. That's the trouble. I can see what they think. They just think I'm an hysterical girl."

"Well, I don't," said Worrals softly. "First of all, let us run over the known facts; you correct me if I've got anything wrong. On May the tenth, a fortnight ago last Saturday, Doris went off duty at five o'clock. About six o'clock she went out for a walk —alone. She did not return. In due course she was posted absent without leave. On Sunday, May the eighteenth, her body was found in the River Ouse by a boy fishing. At the inquest, as there was no evidence to show how she died, and there were no marks of violence on her body, the coroner returned a verdict of 'found drowned,' which in the circumstances was all he could do."

Norma nodded. "I suppose so."

"Tell me," went on Worrals. "You were also off duty on the Saturday evening, or Saturday night, when Doris was last seen alive—were you not?"

"Yes."

"If you were such good friends why didn't you go out together?"

"We always did go out together, but on this particular evening we had arranged to meet two friends, two R.A.F. boys, to go to the pictures. Doris decided not to come as there was something else she wanted to do; so she asked me to meet the boys to wash
66

out the picture arrangement, rather than leave them there waiting."

"What was this something else that Doris wanted to do? Did she tell you what it was?" inquired Worrals.

"Yes. I told the C.O., and the jury, about it, but I could see they didn't attach any importance to it."

"Suppose you tell me about it?" suggested Worrals.

Norma went on. "The thing that cost Doris her life started a month ago. That was on a Saturday night, too. We were on duty at our usual post, Number Fourteen Site, manning the barrage balloon——"

"Where is this post exactly?" interposed Worrals.

"It's on the marshes towards the coast, about three miles from here. It's a sort of shallow valley with the river running through it. They think the Nazis sometimes use the river as a landmark, and fly up it before turning south to attack London from the north. That's why the balloon was put there."

"How long has this particular post been there?"

"At the time I'm talking about the balloon had been there three weeks."

"I see," said Worrals. "Go on."

"It was a cold dark night. There was a moon, but a strong west wind was blowing a lot of low cloud across the sky so that visibility was pretty poor. I've been on balloons for nearly two years so I knew that with that wind blowing if the Nazis came over we were likely to have a wild night of it. The valley runs east to west, and the wind fairly whistles through it. I had just spoken to Doris, who was on the winch, when the alert went."

"What time was this?"

"Ten o'clock."

"Go on."

Norma continued: "Well, nothing much happened. We got the all-clear just after eleven, and about a quarter of an hour later we got orders to pack up. There seemed to be a hitch getting the balloon in. I thought nothing of it, but when Doris came down she told me that an extraordinary thing had happened. She said the balloon suddenly began to swing. She looked up to see what was wrong, and at that moment the moon showed through the clouds. She said she distinctly saw what she thought was a part of the balloon breaking away. There seemed to be a sort of lump hanging on it. Then the lump broke away. Yet the funny thing was, when we got the balloon down there was absolutely nothing wrong with it."

"Did Doris report this incident?" inquired Worrals.

"Oh yes. She reported it to the section officer."

"What happened?"

"Nothing. At least, nothing that I ever heard of."

"I see. What next?"

"Well, ten days later exactly the same thing happened again. The conditions were the same. The wind was blowing the same way and there was an alert. After it was all over Doris shouted to me to look up. I looked and I saw what seemed to be a big bulge under the balloon. Then it broke away and disappeared on the wind into the darkness."

"So you both saw it this time?"

"Yes. But as before there was nothing wrong with the balloon. In the morning I went with Doris and we had a good look at it, but all we could find was a sort of graze, as if the aluminium paint had been

68

scratched. Doris said she was sure that something had collided with the balloon when it was up, and that wasn't the first time it had happened."

"Did she report this?"

"Yes, ma'am; of course; but we heard no more about it. I suppose most girls would have forgotten all about the affair, but Doris wasn't like that. She thought of it a lot. On the afternoon of the Saturday when she disappeared she said to me, something hit our balloon and I'm going to find out what it was. I asked her how she hoped to do that. She said, as the thing—whatever it was—had no engine, or we should have heard it, it must have been travelling on the wind. As the wind was due west the thing could only have come from the west. She said it couldn't have come very far, either, or it would have been higher."

"How did she work that out?" queried Worrals.

"Well, the thing wasn't an aircraft—we were agreed on that. It was round, as if it might have been an old-fashioned free balloon, but smaller. It had a thing, a sort of box, hanging under it."

"Was this box big enough to hold a man?"

"Oh no. I don't think the balloon was big enough either. Doris was sure it was a balloon. If it was, she said, it must have been filled with gas to get it to go up; and if it was filled with gas it couldn't have come far or it would have been higher, even allowing for what we know about the down-current of air in the valley. That's how Doris worked it out, so on the Saturday she went off to do a bit of exploring, as she said, on the west side of our site. I should have gone with her, but, as I told you, we had a date with two boys, and I went along to tell

E

them that we weren't going to the pictures after all. After I had seen them I came home and waited for Doris to come back, but she never came. Even then I had a feeling that something had happened to her. When it came to midnight and she wasn't back I was sure of it. I've never known her to stay out late."

"What is your personal opinion of what did happen to her?" asked Worrals quietly.

Norma looked up almost defiantly. "I think she found what she went to look for. I don't know what it was, but she found it. Spies or fifth columnists are up to something and she discovered what it was. They caught her and killed her and threw her body in the river."

"There were no marks of violence on her body, remember."

"They could have held her face under water to make it look like an accident," argued Norma. "Anyway, of this I am certain. Doris didn't kill herself. When she went out she was perfectly happy. And as I have told you, as she could swim, she could hardly have been drowned by accident, even if she had fallen in the river."

"Does this river, the Ouse, run west to east, through the valley?"

"Yes."

Worrals unfolded a one inch scale ordnance map and spread it on the desk. "Can you show me the exact spot where the body was found?"

"Yes," answered Norma without hesitation. She studied the map for a moment, then pointed. "There —just where this little stream, the Niddy, flows into the Ouse."

"On which bank?"

"This side—that is, the north side."

"Show me the balloon site."

Norma moved her finger. "There."

"Then the body was found about four miles due west of the balloon site?"

"Yes."

Worrals slowly folded the map. "Thank you, Norma. Is that all? I mean, you are absolutely sure there is nothing else we ought to know?"

"I can't think of anything else, ma'am."

"All right," returned Worrals. "I shall go thoroughly into this. If I need you again I'll get in touch with you. I suppose you'll be here?"

"Yes. I'm due for leave, but I'd rather wait now to see what happens. Will you let me know if anything turns up?"

"I will," promised Worrals. "Don't worry. If there *is* dirty work going on we shall find it."

"But don't forget what happened to Doris. She found it."

"Be sure we shall bear that in mind," answered Worrals. "That's all for now."

"Thank you, ma'am." Norma saluted and went out.

Worrals sat still for a few minutes, deep in thought. Then she went through to the outer office. Addressing the adjutant she said with a smile: "Thanks, you can tell the C.O. we've finished with his office."

"Do you want transport?" asked the officer.

"No, thanks. We got a car from East Weald to bring us over. The driver's waiting. Cheerho."

As they left the headquarters Frecks asked: "Are we going straight home?"

"No," decided Worrals. "We'll go back to the airfield and get the machine. I have a fancy to give this district the once-over from topsides—particularly the area due west of Number Fourteen Balloon Site. We should just have time for a quick look round before dark."

II

In rather less than half an hour, flying at a thousand feet, they were cruising in their Communication Squadron Tiger Moth over the broad region of the tragedy. Worrals struck the river nearer to the coast and then, on a westerly course, flew up the shallow valley to which Norma Day had referred. This took the aircraft over the balloon site. They saw the balloon on the ground, with the girls who formed the crew standing by. A minute later the aircraft bumped so violently that Worrals, after she had recovered control, remarked on it to Frecks.

"My word! That was a vicious sinker,* if you like."

"Never mind sinker, I'd call it a stinker," returned Frecks indignantly. "If it hadn't been for my safety belt I should have been left floating in space."

"Then you won't be surprised to learn that we lost two hundred feet of height in it," answered Worrals. "And this is a powered aircraft, remember. I wouldn't have missed it for anything."

"Why not?"

"Because it helps to confirm that girl's story," asserted Worrals. "Unless there was a man in it to unload ballast a free balloon hitting that baby would

* A "sinker is flying slang for a down-current of air.

72

go down like a brick. Of course, anyone releasing free balloons after dark wouldn't know about it; even if they knew about the barrage balloon farther on they would suppose that their own particular gasbag would clear it. Keep your eyes open."

Frecks surveyed the panorama. It was one of those delightful evenings of late spring, clear, warm, with practically no wind; but, nevertheless, there was nothing very attractive about the countryside. To the eastward it consisted almost entirely of flat salt marshes through which several rivers, of which the Ouse was one, wound a meandering course. Looking westward the landscape was somewhat better, the marshes giving way reluctantly to farmland—meadows in which cattle were grazing, and an occasional field of young corn. Trees also appeared, mostly oak or elm, sometimes as small woods, sometimes as solitary trees standing in the hedgerows that separated the fields. There were a few houses, but they were either farms or labourers cottages. The general impression was of a bleak loneliness, lacking the life, colour and atmosphere of activity usually to be found in rural districts at no great distance from London. One area provided the exception. This was a fairly extensive stretch of parkland well furnished with stately trees; almost in the centre, amid ornamental trees and shrubs, stood a house of some size, the type that a house agent might with justification have described as a stately Elizabethan mansion.

Frecks had concentrated her attention on this prominent landmark when Worrals called her attention to the river, pointing out its confluence with a tributary.

"That little river must be the Niddy," said Worrals.

"It was there, at the junction, among those rushes on the far bank, that Doris Marchant's body was found. The Niddy seems to pass extraordinarily close to that big house. What's the name of it? Does it give it on your map?"

Frecks, who had the map on her knees, consulted it. "Gresham Grange," she announced.

"The garden seems to be in a bit of a mess. I imagine there's nobody there; too close to Bomb Alley, perhaps, as the Nazis are rather given to coming in this way."

"I think there's somebody there," replied Frecks. "I saw a man on the roof a minute ago."

"On the roof?" Surprise lifted Worrals' voice a tone. "People don't usually stand on their roofs."

"There was somebody on that flat part a minute ago," asserted Frecks. "I can't see him now. The place may be an Observer Corps post, or a Civil Defence unit. A lot of big houses have been taken over by the government for that purpose."

Worrals did not answer. She had dropped a wing to get a better view of the house.

"Why not go closer and have a good look at it?" suggested Frecks.

"And tell the people there that they're under observation?" asked Worrals sarcastically. "Not likely."

She flew on a little way making a close reconnaissance of the landscape, mile by mile. At last she said: "Well, I can't see anything to get excited about. The light's going—we'd better be getting back. That little town on the horizon to the north must be Burnham. I don't think we need bother about it." She brought the aircraft round in a wide turn and started back over her course.

74

"Were you looking for anything in particular?" inquired Frecks.

"No," replied Worrals. "I thought we might see something, but I don't know what. No matter; the trip's been worth while if only because we've now got a clear picture of the country—a better picture than we could get from the map. The only thing of interest was that big house. If there is anything funny going on that might be the spot; but I only say that because there's nowhere else—at least, as far as I could see."

Worrals flew back to the airfield, landing in the deceptive light of dusk, handed the machine over to the maintenance section and walked on to the squadron office.

The station adjutant looked up with a smile. "Everything okay?"

"More or less," returned Worrals vaguely. "What's the met* report?"

"There's a cold front coming from the west. It should reach here about eleven o'clock."

"Wind and rain?"

"Probably. But it's a narrow front and should soon pass over."

Worrals changed the subject. "Are you expecting an alert to-night?"

The adjutant smiled wanly. "The weather's right for one."

"Mind of I use your phone?" asked Worrals.

"Not at all."

Worrals spoke to the telephone operator. "Get me the police station at Burnham," she ordered. When the connection was made she went on. "Is

* Service abreviation for meteorological.

that Burnham police station? This is Squadron Officer Worralson, W.A.A.F., speaking from the R.A.F. station at East Weald. I'd like to have a word with the inspector, please—oh, that is the inspector. Good. I'm speaking for the Air Ministry. We're expecting a big intake of personnel here and I'm looking for accommodation. I see from the map that there's a biggish place in your area called Gresham Grange. I suppose it doesn't happen by any chance to be unoccupied? It is. Yes . . . yes . . . yes. Suppose I want to look at the place, is there anyone to show me over? Not even a caretaker? I see. . . . Who lived there before these people took over? . . . By the way, is the house in pretty good repair? I mean, has it been damaged by bombs, or anything like that? Ah-huh. I see. . . . Much obliged, inspector. Good night." Worrals hung up, threw a smile of thanks at the adjutant and touched Frecks on the arm. "Let's go and get something to eat," she suggested.

As soon as they were outside the office Frecks demanded: "What was all that about?"

"I rang up the police thinking I might learn something," answered Worrals. "They keep a pretty close watch on things nowadays."

"Did you learn anything?"

"Plenty. In the first place, the house is unoccupied, but it might be, because it was taken over early in the war by a London firm of stockbrokers in case their city offices were blitzed. As they haven't taken up residence we may assume that the London offices are still intact. All the same, that strikes me as a bit odd. When the blitz started most city firms with country accommodation evacuated their staffs without waiting for the roof to fall in on them. The staff got a chance to get some sleep then. Apparently this firm thinks differently. Anyhow, the place is empty —not even a caretaker."

"But I tell you I saw a man on the roof," insisted Frecks.

"Talking of the roof, I can tell you something about that, too," resumed Worrals. "Just before the war, before the present people had the place, the Grange was taken by a stargazer—astronomer, if you like. He spent a lot of money having a sliding roof fitted so that he could sit upstairs and spy on the stars through a big telescope. Observatories are built like that, I believe."

Frecks stared. "An arrangement like that would be useful to some people—with a war on," she said slowly.

Worrals smiled. "I hadn't overlooked that."

"What was that talk about bombs?" queried Frecks.

"Just an idea I had on the spur of the moment," returned Worrals. "After all, if it should so happen that the Nazis have an interest in Gresham Grange they'd hardly be likely to knock the place about with bombs, would they?"

"No."

"Well, that's how it is. Of course, it may be coincidence but although Burnham's had plenty of bombs, and quite a few have been broadcast round about, so far not a single bomb has fallen in Gresham park. From which we may conclude that either the park is lucky—or else enemy bombers have been told to watch where they're throwing their bombs when they're in the vicinity of Gresham Grange. We may be barking up the wrong tree," went on Worrals, "but here we have several coincidences in a row, and I don't altogether trust coincidence. When you get a spate of coincidences the thing becomes worth investigating."

"From which I gather you intend to investigate Gresham Grange?"

"That's the idea," stated Worrals. "Apart from what I've told you, the Grange happens to be the only place of any size due west of Number Fourteen Balloon Site. It's also worth noting that the River Niddy passes very close to it. We've no proof that Doris Marchant ever went near the place, but on the other hand, we don't know that she didn't. Her body either came down the Ouse or down the Niddy. It might have been one or the other, but if I had to bet on it, in view of what we know now, I'd put my money on the Niddy. If the body came down that little river the current could easily carry it across to the far bank of the Ouse. One thing and another I feel like having a closer look at Gresham Grange."

"When are we going on this jaunt?"

"To-night. The conditions are right. The place isn't far from here. We'll requisition a car and go along as soon as we've had dinner. By the way, put a pistol in your pocket. I shall take one. We may feel silly if we don't need them—but not as silly as we should if he did need them and hadn't got them. Doris Marchant went for a stroll in the same direction and she didn't come back. I aim to come back; at least, I shall be prepared to argue with anyone who tries to stop me."

Frecks looked dubious. "Suppose something fishy *is* going on at the Grange? Do you think we're capable of handling it? I'm all against biting off more than we can chew."

Worrals thought for a moment before she answered. "There is a chance that we may run into a rough house—that's obvious, or I shouldn't be going. If Doris Marchant was in fact murdered we may take it that a mistake on our part, such as she made, would see us sharing her dismal fate. I'd hate that to happen. To reduce the chances of that, it might be a good thing to have a safety valve if things go wrong—a line of communication, so to speak, with outside assistance."

"That means bringing someone else into the affair."

"It does, and I think I know the right person. Norma Day. She struck me as a girl who takes her nerve with her, and she has, moreover, a personal interest. If she knew for sure that Doris Marchant had been murdered, if she could get her hands on the people who did it she'd tear their eyes out. That's the sort of person we want. I'll ring up her C.O. and arrange for her to have the night off. We'll pick her up on the way. She can stand a little way off and watch events. If we don't come back there will be at least one person who knows where we disappeared. Let's go in and eat."

III

It was nearly nine o'clock when Worrals drove out past the guard at the main gate. "The met people were right about the weather," she observed after a glance at the sky. "It's deteriorating. I hope it doesn't get *too* dark."

79

In twenty minutes they had reached the balloon unit where they found Norma Day waiting. Worrals spoke to her seriously.

"Now listen," she said. "This is the position. We know very little more than when we saw you this afternoon. We've had a look round from the air, but there wasn't much to see. There is only one big house, a place called Gresham Grange. That's our objective. There may be nothing there, or there may be something. We don't know; that's why we're going, to find out. I'm taking you with us because, in the first place, you can help us, and secondly, because you have a personal interest in this business. You won't actually come to the Grange with us; you will stand at a place I shall decide, and your job will be to keep watch, so that should we get into difficulties you will be in a position to fetch help. I have a Very pistol in my pocket. If we get in a jam I shall fire a red light. If you see a red light, streak for Wing Headquarters and see the wing commander. I've spoken to him on the phone. He will at once get into touch with our chief at the Air Ministry, to whom I have also spoken. He knows what we're doing and is standing by until the matter is cleared up. The wing commander tells me you can drive a car—is that correct?"

"Yes. I applied for enlistment as a driver, but the group was full up."

"That's fine. We shall leave you with the car while we go forward on foot to explore. If you see a red light go to the wing commander. If we're not back in two hours you'll go to him anyhow. Is that clear?"

"Perfectly," answered Norma. Her manner was one of grim satisfaction.

"All right, let's get along," said Worrals, getting into the driving seat and starting the engine.

Ten minutes saw them at the park boundary, a comparatively new brick wall high enough to prevent anyone on the road from overlooking the park. By standing on the step of the car, however, it was possible to see over. Beyond the wall, at the bottom of a sloping grass field, was the river Ouse, a dark, turgid, reed-fringed stream, perhaps forty yards wide.

Worrals switched off the car light, cruised on a little way, and then allowed the vehicle to run quietly to a standstill. "This should suit us," she murmured. "As I remember it we're about two hundred yards from the place where the Niddy joins the main river. You can see the chimneys of the Grange, Norma, against the sky—rising from that low ground half left. Can you see them?"

"Yes."

"All right. Keep your eyes on that spot. You know what to do?"

"Yes, ma'am."

"Apart from the instructions I've given you you'll have to use your initiative. Naturally, if you hear any considerable noise, such as shooting, you'll go for help, anyway." Worrals looked at Norma critically. "You're not nervous about being left alone?"

"Not in the least," was the firm answer. "All I want is to have a crack at the people who killed Doris."

"That's the spirit," agreed Worrals. "This is what we shall do. We shall get over the wall here, walk down to the river, and follow it to where the Niddy joins it. We shall then turn up the Niddy to the house. Hark!" She raised her head in a listening attitude.

"That's the Burnham siren," stated Norma, as faintly on the breeze came the unmistakable wail.

"Good. I was hoping we should get one," said Worrals.

"Why?" asked Frecks.

"Because, except that the wind isn't so strong, conditions are now precisely the same as when the girls saw something collide with balloon fourteen."

"You think the siren has something to do with it?"

"It might," answered Worrals. "I can't imagine how, unless it's because the siren drives most people to shelter and so reduces the chance of anyone being about to see what goes on here—if anything does go on. Or it may be that enemy agents have to operate a visual signalling device which would only be of any use if German aircraft were overhead. Anyhow, it sounds as if Jerry is coming this way—I can hear guns in the distance. Let's go."

She climbed the wall and went on down the slope towards the river. Frecks caught up with her. Reaching the water Worrals gazed at it for a moment or two before continuing along the bank. "It must have been along here that Doris Marchant came the night she lost her life," she remarked.

"What happened to her might happen to us," sugested Frecks.

"That is what I'm hoping will happen—that is, up to a point," replied Worrals coolly. "The end should work out differently though. Doris was alone, and unarmed. She wasn't ready for trouble. We are."

She went on and did not speak again until they

reached the junction of the Niddy with the main river. The Niddy was a much smaller stream, but like the Ouse it flowed deep and dark through reed-lined banks. Its movement, however, was less sluggish.

Worrals stopped and pointed to the far bank. "Doris's body was found somewhere over there. It could of course have come down the Ouse, but if it did, why did it stop there? On the other hand, if it came down the Niddy the current would probably carry it right across the main stream to the far bank—where those dead sticks and things are lying. I'd say they came down the Niddy. We can easily test it. Find a piece of wood. There should be plenty under those trees behind us."

It did not take them long to find a stout piece of dead wood. Worrals swung it out into the middle of the smaller stream. They watched. For a little while it hardly moved; then it drifted on towards the confluence. Worrals sat down. Frecks sat beside her and together they gazed at the piece of flotsam while it went on across the main river to run ashore against the rushes of the far bank.

"I imagine a body, afloat or under water, would behave in much the same way," observed Worrals quietly. "Come on, it's getting chilly."

"Just a minute." With face upturned Frecks laid a restraining hand on Worrals' arm. "What's this coming? It isn't one of our machines. That motor has a nasty Nazi growl to it. Sounds to me like a Messer 109 going flat out."

They stood still while the aircraft came on, to pass almost directly overhead.

"Watch the house for lights," said Worrals crisply.

They watched.

"Did I, or did I not, see a sort of faint reflection on one of those chimney stacks as the machine went over?" murmured Frecks.

"I thought I saw something, but I wouldn't swear to it," returned Worrals. "In the dark the imagination can sometimes see things that aren't there."

The aircraft passed on, and presently dancing flecks of anti-aircraft fire showed that the outer gun defences were in action. The flecks grew brighter.

"That machine's coming back; the guns are following it," declared Frecks.

"It is. The pilot soon got fed up with being shot at, didn't he? Or maybe he's done what he was sent over to do. But it's no use guessing about that. Let's get on."

Worrals set off, now following the bank of the smaller river.

A few minutes walk brought them to the Grange, revealed clearly by the outline of roof and chimney stacks against the sky. Worrals went on until they were brought to a stop by a low iron fence which made a dividing line between the gardens of the house and the park.

"According to the police this place is empty," murmured Worrals. "There's no one in it at all— not a soul. Yet you say you saw a man on the roof this afternoon. Somebody's making a mistake."

"I'm old enough to know a man when I see one," declared Frecks with asperity.

"Okay—okay," put in Worrals quietly.

"I wouldn't be sure, but it struck me that he behaved as if he had heard our engine and bobbed

84

out to have a look at us. Seeing we were low he bobbed back again."

"If there was a man there this afternoon it seems likely that he's still there," said Worrals.

"Unless he was a plumber or a workman doing repairs."

"There would be no need for a plumber to bob back when he saw us. He'd be more likely to wave," Worrals pointed out. "But guessing won't get us anywhere. Let's get some facts."

"Does that mean you're going into the house?"

"Probably."

"How are you going to get in?"

"There are two ways of gaining admittance to a house," replied Worrals. "One can go to the front door like a respectable caller and ring the bell, or one can get in through a window like a burglar. In this case ringing the bell would obviously defeat our object, so it looks as if it will have to be the other way. Let's——" She broke off abruptly, gripping Frecks' arm. She pointed. "Look! What's that! On the roof."

Following the direction indicated by Worrals' outstretched finger Frecks saw that something had altered. The outline of the roof was different. Now, silhouetted against the sky where before there had been a flat roof, appeared a dome, a dome that slowly grew larger until it became a sphere. Then, suddenly, it shot upwards at an oblique angle in an easterly direction and was lost to view in the darkness.

"That thing came from the place where I saw the man this afternoon," breathed Frecks. "What was it?"

"I don't know—beyond the obvious fact that it

F

was a balloon of some sort," answered Worrals. "The point is, it's the thing we're looking for. It's the thing, or one like it, that has twice collided with our barrage balloon. The girls were right in their description of it. Did you see the box affair hanging underneath?"

"Of course."

"Travelling on a west wind that balloon will in due course arrive over Holland or Germany," said Worrals in a low voice. "The basket, or box, or whatever it was, wasn't big enough to carry a man; nor was the balloon for that matter; but it might carry smaller things—papers, for instance."

"But suppose it was carrying messages to Germany; how would the Germans get hold of it?" questioned Frecks.

"I was just thinking about that," replied Worrals. "I don't think it would be very difficult. For instance, if that box affair carried a delayed action lamp, one that flashed a pre-arranged signal, its recovery would be a simple matter. Watchers would spot it as soon as it crossed the enemy coast and a pilot could be sent up to shoot it down. But that's guessing again. Doris Marchant was right, Frecks. She worked the problem out very much as we have. In her determination to solve the mystery she went a bit too far and lost her life."

"Don't let us make the same blunder," advised Frecks earnestly. "Let's go home and report."

"I'm inclined to agree with you," said Worrals. "All the same, I feel that somebody ought to keep an eye on the place in case anything else happens. I'll tell you what. I'll stay here and keep watch. You slip back to Norma and tell her to do her stuff.

Tell her to report what we've seen to the wing commander, who must get in touch with the air commodore. She might say that we have good reason to suspect that Gresham Grange is being used as an operating base by enemy agents, so will he please take the necessary action as quickly as possible. We are standing by to keep the place under observation, and perhaps make a closer reconnaissance. As soon as Norma has gone you come back and join me here. When Norma has delivered her message she had better bring the car back to the rendezvous and keep an eye open for us. Okay. Get cracking."

Frecks went off at the double.

IV

After Frecks had disappeared Worrals settled down to pass the time by watching the roof in front of her in case there should be a repetition of the sinister incident they had just witnessed; but she saw nothing, and heard nothing except a distant all-clear siren.

From her position by the garden fence she could only see for a very short distance up the river, which puzzled her, for it seemed to disappear abruptly. From time to time a young moon bleared mistily through clouds that now threatened rain, and on one such occasion, taking advantage of the improved visibility, she walked on a few yards, taking care not to lose sight of the rendezvous. She soon discovered why the river could not be seen. It disappeared under a rough timber bridge. She noticed, too, that the river had been confined within banks of brickwork so that it took the form of a canal rather than a river. In this artificial conduit the water was a good two feet below the level of the ground on either side. The brick banks, too, had been brought closer to each other, with the result that the water moved at a fair speed. The reason for this treatment of the water was not apparent, unless, pondered Worrals, it had been used higher up to drive a turbine to provide the house with electric power, perhaps for lighting purposes. Or, she thought, it might have been to reduce dampness in the house or to prevent erosion of the banks close to the house when the river was in spate. Considering the matter she was inclined to the latter view, for looking up the water she observed that it passed so close to the walls of the Grange as almost to form a moat. A little higher up, near what she imagined must be the front of the house, was the bridge, a narrow ornamental affair in the style usually called rustic. All this Worrals noted carefully, because in view of what they had just seen she became more and more convinced that the building, and its direct water link with the Ouse, was associated with the unfortunate girl who had lost her life. Deep in thought she turned back towards the rendezvous; but she had not taken half-a-dozen steps when an unseen door scraped, no great distance away. She stared in the direction from which the sound had come, but she could see nothing on account of the dense shadow cast by the building and the surrounding trees. Not daring to delay she hastened back just in time to see Frecks coming.

"What news?" greeted Worrals. "Talk fast. I think something is happening at the house."

"It's okay," whispered Frecks. "Norma went

off some minutes ago. She's coming back to the same place as soon as she's made contact with the wing commander. How long do you think it will be before reinforcements arrive?"

"I imagine that will depend on where Raymond sends them from," answered Worrals. "He didn't tell me what he had in mind, but as he knows what we're doing his plan should be cut and dried, so I shall be surprised if someone isn't here in twenty minutes or half an hour at the outside. No matter. I feel easier in my mind now I know he's on the move. I've been looking at the river. A bit farther on the banks have been bricked up. If Doris Marchant fell in, or was pushed in, anywhere near the house, she'd have a job to get out. Presently you'll see for yourself what I mean. I think we might now risk going a bit nearer. We'll take it slowly. No noise. Someone is moving about. I heard a door scrape a minute ago—it sounded as if someone had dragged open a garage door."

Moving slowly and with extreme caution they walked nearer to the house, Worrals leading, keeping close to the water. Once she paused to look at a place where the bank had fallen in to form a little sandy beach, but she made no comment. After continuing for a little way she paused again to indicate with a jerk of her thumb the walled banks of the river to which she had referred. On their right, only a few paces distant, now loomed the black bulk of the house. Not a light showed anywhere. They went on again and so reached the rustic bridge, which Worrals now observed led to a small summerhouse. On their right was the front of the house, faced by a broad macadam area, from which the main drive, also macadam, ran on to disappear in an avenue of tall elms.

Worrals touched Frecks on the arm and whispered: "There doesn't seem any point in going farther. There's the front door. I imagine our reinforcements will come up the drive—or some of them will. We'll wait here."

They waited for some time. Once, for a little while, voices could be heard talking in low tones; but they could not be located.

"That proves the police have been misinformed about the place being unoccupied," breathed Worrals. "Evidently that man you saw on the roof wasn't alone."

Shortly after this there was a metallic clang from somewhere not far away.

"That sounded like the bonnet of a car being closed," whispered Frecks.

"I think so," answered Worrals. And hardly had the words left her lips when a starter whirred, to be followed by the hum of an engine.

"They've got a car here," murmured Worrals. "I'm afraid they're going to use it. I fancy that explains why the drive is macadam instead of gravel, as is more usual in a place like this. Macadam doesn't show wheel tracks. Gravel would—and the police might wonder. I hope Raymond isn't going to be much longer. I've got an uncomfortable feeling that these birds are going to flit. They may not live here, but use it only as an operating base. That's a possibility I hadn't thought of. If they go we've no means of following, so we may lose them yet."

These suspicions were soon confirmed. A big saloon car, showing no lights, came quietly round the far end of the house, apparently from the garage, and pulled up before the front door. There it remained with the engine running.

The moment it appeared Worrals had backed into a small group of evergreen shrubs, pulling Frecks with her. "This is awkward," she breathed.

"What are we going to do about it?" queried Frecks.

"Nothing for the moment—except keep still and quiet," returned Worrals. "We'll see what happens."

"But you're not going to let them get away?"

Worrals hesitated. "It's awkward," she repeated. "We can't start shooting people on the mere suspicion of their being enemy agents. *Ssh*. Quiet."

A man, walking quickly, had come round the corner whence the car had appeared. Reaching the vehicle he stopped and spoke to someone in it. A door swung open, and from the car stepped a burly figure, wearing an overcoat with the collar turned up. There was a brief conversation; then one of the men rapped sharply on the front door. A few seconds passed and this door was opened. Two men emerged. It was too dark for features to be distinguished. In fact, it was too dark for anything to be seen clearly beyond the fact that there were now four men by the car. Then one of them spoke, harshly, briefly, and at the sound Frecks felt Worrals stiffen. She knew why. The language used was German. One of the others answered in the same tongue, and got into the car.

"They're going," breathed Frecks.

"Not if I know it," said Worrals through her teeth. She went on, quickly, tersely. "Only Germans would speak German, and Germans have no right to be floating loose at a place and time like this. Raymond should be here any minute. We've got to prevent that car from leaving. I'm going for the tyres. Here, take the Very pistol. It's loaded. The moment I open fire send up the red light. Things are liable to happen; there isn't much cover here, but it's the best available so stick to it." She thrust the Very pistol into Frecks' hand, ran out to put the car between her and the men at the door, and closed to within three yards of it.

Quick as she was, a cry of alarm in a male voice warned her that she had been seen. Cutting into it came the *bang—bang—bang* of her automatic. Mingled with the reports came the hiss of air escaping under pressure. This in turn was punctuated by a heavy report and a flash as Frecks sent the red light skywards.

Things continued to happen quickly; so quickly in fact, that for the next few seconds Frecks found it hard to keep pace with them. Worrals, having achieved her object of disabling the car dashed back into cover; but in the lurid glow of the red light she was seen, for now that the men had recovered from the initial shock of surprise they were not idle. Two spurts of flame leapt from the group, and two bullets ripping through the bushes near her head were enough to make Frecks drop flat. She fired two answering shots rather wildly, but had the satisfaction of seeing one of the men fall. Another, firing as he ran, bravely but foolishly charged the bushes. Flame and a trail of sparks leapt from the muzzle of Worrals' gun; they ended at the man's chest; he stumbled and fell. More shots came from the door, whence now came angry cries. A car door slammed. The engine revved.

Then, suddenly, it shot upwards at an oblique angle in an easterly direction and was lost to view in the darkness.

The car bumped a foot or two, then stopped. A man jumped out of it and dived for the front door of the house. Worrals took a snap shot at him and missed. Another shot came smacking through the thick leaves of the shrubs.

"Where's Raymond?" muttered Frecks, in something like a panic. "Why doesn't he come?"

"He'll come," answered Worrals in a brittle voice. "Keep low. Fire at the flashes. The car's no use. We've got two of them . We can stop the others from leaving the house by *this* door, anyway."

Another bullet came ripping through the bushes.

Frecks fired at the flash, but could not see if the shot had any effect.

A curious attentive silence fell. The red glow faded suddenly as the charge became exhausted, leaving the scene to a disconcerting darkness. Straining her eyes Frecks could just see a man on his knees, on the doorstep. He was groaning, and coughing between groans.

"Where are the rest?" she whispered to Worrals.

"I think they've backed into the house," answered Worrals. "I hope they'll stay there, but I'm afraid they won't. These bushes are too flimsy for my liking. The trouble is, the men know where we are."

"Then let's get out," urged Frecks.

"We can't leave without exposing ourselves," objected Worrals. "Besides, I want to keep that door covered." She pressed herself flat against the earth as more shots tore through the bushes, and was rising to answer the fire when a stream of shots came from a new direction. The bullets thudded viciously into the ground, one of them close enough to spurt earth into her face.

93

"Those shots are coming from upstairs," she said, alarm in her voice.

"There's a man on the roof almost above us," answered Frecks, lying flat as more shots came down.

"We've got to get out of this," decided Worrals. "It's getting too hot."

"Let's make a bolt for it."

"Not into the open. What's behind us?"

"The river."

More shots crashed through the bushes, both from the front door and the roof. Something plucked at Worrals' sleeve. "I'd rather get my shirt wet than have a bullet through it," she said in a tense voice. "I'm for the river. Come on." She began edging backwards through the bushes.

She had not far to go. The water looked cold, black, evil, but she slid into it, keeping her head and arms above water by hanging on to the bank. "Hold on to the bank," she warned Frecks.

"Why doesn't Raymond come?" muttered Frecks irritably, and as she spoke three more shots came tearing through the bushes. She uttered a cry of pain and pitched forward, falling on Worrals, whose grip on the bank was broken. In a moment they were both being carried down the stream.

Worrals dropped her legs and got a shock when they failed to touch bottom. She had no idea the water was so deep. Swimming, she grasped Frecks by the tunic, although in order to do this she had to abandon her pistol. Frecks struggled feebly, muttering incoherently.

Worrals struck out for the bank, and she did in fact reach it, but the bricked-up sides through which they were now passing were covered with slimy weed and offered no hand-hold. Still clinging to Frecks, the water carried them both along. The dark mass of the house slid past. Someone was shouting, but her position was too desperate for her to pay heed to it.

The water was icy cold. Worrals felt her strength going, so she abandoned everything to the task of saving herself and Frecks. Several times she was able to touch the bank, but always the brick sides threw her back into the current, and in this way they were swept along. Even at that dire moment the thought flashed into her mind that this was what must have happened to Doris Marchant. Then a gleam of moonlight showed her something that she had forgotten. It was the little sandy beach where the bank had broken down that she had noted on the way up. Exerting her last ounce of strength she splashed towards it. Her feet struck the bottom. Half swimming, half wading, stumbling and falling, she struggled up the beach, dragging Frecks behind her. Panting, she pulled Frecks clear of the water and then sank down, fighting for breath, for she was nearly spent. Subconsciously she was aware of a noise of shooting and shouting in the direction of the house; but she was too concerned about Frecks to even look. There was blood on Frecks' face.

Frecks gasped, and struggled weakly, trying to get up. "What is it—where are we?" she muttered.

"Where did you get it?" asked Worrals.

"In the face. Something hit my face." Frecks managed to get into a sitting position.

Worrals was relieved and astonished, for it was evident that the wound was less serious than she

95

had every reason to suppose. But before she could express her relief, or, in fact, before she could do anything, she heard footsteps thumping, and looking up she saw a man running along the river bank from the direction of the house. Apparently he saw them at the same time, for he let out a grunt of satisfaction.

It did not take Worrals long to perceive that this new peril was more deadly than the last. Yet it seemed that there was nothing she could do. She had lost her automatic and she had no other weapon. A feeling of helplessness surged through her. "Frecks, have you still got your gun?" she asked urgently.

"No," answered Frecks.

"The Very pistol?"

"No."

Worrals looked up to see the man towering over them. She could see the stub outline of an automatic as he raised his right hand. Instinctively she turned and half rose to meet the attack. Her hands were on sand. She suddenly realized it. Her fingers sank into it. With a swift movement she scooped up a handful, and a split second before the pistol blazed flung it at the man's face with all the force she could muster. Apparently the sand achieved its object, for the bullet went wide, *plunking* into the water.

Cursing luridly in German the man staggered back a pace wiping his face with his left arm. Worrals flung more sand, but this time the man was ready and he only laughed unpleasantly. Again the pistol came up. Worrals saw it. She saw something else. Someone, quite close, was running across the field towards them. She had no idea who it was. Nor did she care. She let out a shrill cry for help.

The man laughed again and took a step nearer, presumably to make sure this time of hitting his target. This, in the event, was his undoing, for even as he took deliberate aim the running figure arrived on the scene. Worrals was amazed to see that it was a girl. "Look out!" she cried. "He's got a gun!"

The girl did not stop. She took what is commonly called a running jump. Her weight struck the man full in the back, and the result was definite and instantaneous. He was hurtled forward. The pistol flew out of his hand and he went headlong into the river with a resounding splash. The girl came on to Worrals who by this time was on her feet, staring incredulously as she recognized the new arrival.

"Norma!" she cried. "What's happened?"

"I saw the red light so I came to see if I could help," answered Norma simply.

"What about the troops?" asked Worrals.

"Judging from the din they've arrived at the house," replied Norma. "Who's that?" she went on quickly, pointing at the man who was now trying to drag himself up the opposite bank.

"He's one of the gang who killed Doris Marchant," replied Worrals.

"Is he though?" Norma's voice was grim. She started looking for something on the ground, although curiously enough Worrals did not at once realize what it was. She realized it though when Norma suddenly straightened herself and raised her right arm. Flame streamed across the river as the heavy pistol crashed. *Bang—bang—bang* roared the weapon.

"Hi! That's enough," shouted Worrals, as the

97

man slid slowly back into the water. Worrals watched, but he did not reappear.

Norma flung the pistol into the turbulent water that marked the place where he had vanished. "Take that," she muttered viciously.

"All right—he's had it," said Worrals. "Go easy. What's happened at the house—as far as you know?"

"I don't know anything about it," answered Norma. "All I know is, about six tenders went roaring past me on the road. There's been a lot of shooting—and a bomb or two, I think."

"You'd better go up and send an ambulance down here," ordered Worrals. "My friend is a casualty."

"Nothing of the sort," denied Frecks. "I'm all right," she declared, sitting up.

"What happened?" asked Worrals.

"It wasn't a bullet—at least I don't think it could have been," returned Frecks. "I think the bullet knocked off a piece of wood or something which hit me across the face. My face feels pretty tender, but I can't find a hole in it anywhere. Somewhat unsteadily Frecks rose to her feet. "See? I'm okay," she announced.

"You think you can walk up to the house?"

"I could run if I thought there was a hot bath at the end of it," asserted Frecks. "My word! Isn't that water cold? Hello! What's all this coming?" she added quickly, staring up the river bank.

Turning in that direction Worrals saw several men running towards them.

"Is that you, Worrals?" cried a voice, sharp with anxiety.

"Great Scott! It's the big chief himself," said Worrals. "Yes, sir, here we are," she called.

The air commodore ran up. He was accompanied by an officer and some men of the R.A.F. Regiment, armed with rifles.

"Are you all right?" asked the Air Commodore quickly.

"More or less."

"What are you doing here?"

"Getting our breath," answered Worrals. "We've just had a pretty sticky ten minutes. We finished in the river, so if you don't mind we'll get back to quarters and get out of our wet clothes. You might tell me what's happened at the house though."

"We were throwing a cordon round the establishment when your red light went up," stated the Air Commodore. "It sort of speeded our arrangements. We closed in right away. There was a bit of fuss, but it's all over now. We've picked up three dead Nazis and two live ones."

"There's another in the river here," said Worrals. "I think he's dead, in which case his body will probably be washed up where Doris Marchant was found."

"All right. You can leave that to us. You'd better get back to the Balloon Wing right away and get out of those wet clothes. I'll be along to-morrow morning for your reports. By that time I may be able to tell you just what has been going on here."

"Okay, sir." Worrals turned to Norma. "Do you feel like taking us home?"

"Certainly, ma'am."

"Then let's get along," said Worrals.

They set off across the field towards the car.

V

The details of what became known officially as the Gresham Incident were narrated the following morning by Air Commodore Raymond in a private room at the Balloon Wing Headquarters. Worrals, Frecks and Norma had already written their reports. Frecks carried a souvenir of the affair in the shape of a strip of surgical plaster on her cheek.

"How long this business at the Grange has been going on we don't know for certain," said the Air Commodore gravely. "It seems likely that it has been going on for some time, for there are indications that the estate was one of those bases established by the enemy before the war. When we have checked up no doubt we shall find that the so-called astronomer who installed the sliding roof was a German. That macadam drive, which would not show wheel marks, was probably laid at the same time. Even as it was, a lonely estate like the Grange must have suited the enemy admirably. There is no doubt that it had become a serious leak in our defence system. As you probably know, the difficulty of espionage is not, as some people suppose, the collection of useful information. Information is not hard to get. The trouble is, as we ourselves know, to get it out of the country without the method of communication being spotted by counter-espionage experts. That is where most agents—call them spies if you like—eventually slip up, as has happened in this case. Aircraft and parachutes have provided a ready means of placing agents in a country, but the transmission of the information they pick up is not so easy. At Gresham Grange the enemy sprung a new trick on us. But for the chance collisions of his balloons with our barrage balloon it might have gone on for a long time." The Air Commodore lit a cigarette.

"The equipment we have found at the Grange has pretty well told us the story. The rest of what we wanted to know has been supplied by one of the surviving Nazis who, in the hope of escaping the death penalty, has decided to talk. When it was desired to transmit documents the enemy had merely to take advantage of the prevailing wind by releasing a free balloon to which was attached a container in which the documents were placed. In the same way small objects could be sent across the North Sea. Indeed, there is reason to suppose that the Grange was a sort of central registry for several, if not all, of the agents working in this country. By keeping watch we hope to catch some of them when they arrive. In the lower part of the container was an ingenious contrivance—a small radio unit which only went into operation when it came within the influence of the Radar screen installed by the enemy along his frontiers. Entering this screen the radio sent out a persistent call signal which revealed its position. After that it was an easy matter to send up an aircraft to shoot it down. Nevertheless, since it was not known when a balloon was to be launched this involved a lot of work for listening posts, and it was to reduce this labour that a special machine was sent over here during an alert. The pilot's job was to pick up a visual signal from the Grange. This told him the time of launching the balloon. The enemy, knowing the speed of the wind, and its direction, would

G

be able to judge fairly accurately where and when the balloon would arrive. Ingenious but simple. Most of this information we have got from the Nazi spy who, seeing nothing in front of him but a firing party, has lost his nerve."

"So that's how it was done?" murmured Worrals.

"The discovery of the scheme was a nice piece of work on your part," complimented the Air Commodore.

"Not on *my* part," denied Worrals. "Say, on the part of Doris Marchant. To her and her alone belongs the credit. Had it not been for her the Grange would still be functioning as a spy depot; and since for her pains she lost her life I hope you will see that she *does* get the credit, sir. Acknowledgment, too, must be made to Norma Day, for had she not insisted on a further investigation into the death of her friend the thing would soon have been forgotten."

"I shall attend to that," promised the Air Commodore. "I shall be happy to recommend Aircraftwoman Day for a commission if she wants one." He looked at Norma. "You have already the satisfaction of revenge," he went on. "The man you knocked into the river was the man who killed your friend. We know that because the Nazi who is doing the talking has told us all about it, to escape personal responsibility."

"Then that makes our little effort doubly worth while," declared Worrals. "What do you say, Norma?"

Norma smiled. "I agree with you, ma'am. I feel happier now that I know Doris did not die in vain, and that those who killed her have got what they deserve."

"That's the right spirit," concluded the Air Commodore, rising. "I must be getting back to the Ministry."

"Have you got room for three in your car, sir?" asked Worrals.

"Yes—why?"

"Frecks and I are taking Norma out for a spot of lunch in town."

The Air Commodore nodded approval. "Good idea. Let's be going."

STORY

3

THUNDER OVER GERMANY

A "Biggles" Adventure

SQUADRON LEADER BIGGLESWORTH, D.S.O., glanced up from his desk, and broke off in what he was saying to Air Commodore Raymond, of the Air Ministry, as a knock came on the door. "Come in," he said crisply.

The station adjutant entered. "There's a boy outside asking to see you, sir," he reported.

Squadron Leader Bigglesworth, better known in the Royal Air Force as "Biggles," raised his eyebrows. "A boy?"

"Yes, sir. He's been pestering me for the last hour. He says it's something really urgent."

"But I'm in conference with the Air Commodore," Biggles pointed out.

"I've told him that, sir. He really seems to have something on his mind, so I thought I'd better tell you."

"Who is this boy—do you know him?"

"He's one of the Air Training Corps cadets who have been working this morning in the hangars.

They come along once a week, you know, as part of their training."

"Better hear what he has to say, Bigglesworth," put in Air Commodore Raymond, of Air Intelligence. "I don't suppose it's anything really important, but I believe in encouraging these lads as much as possible."

"Very well, sir," acknowledged Biggles. Then, to the adjutant: "Show him in."

The adjutant beckoned to somebody outside, and a moment later a tall, blue-eyed, fair-haired lad marched into the room, halted and saluted. He wore the blue uniform of the Air Training Corps.

"All right—stand at ease," said Biggles in a friendly voice. "What's the trouble?"

"It isn't exactly trouble, sir," answered the cadet, "but there is something important I wish to say —or I think it may be important. I can only get away from my work one day a week, so if I missed this chance I should have to wait for another seven days."

"Couldn't you have spoken to one of the other officers?" queried Biggles.

The boy looked a trifle embarrassed. "Well, I suppose I could, sir; but I've heard so much about you, and your raids over enemy country, that I thought I'd like to report to you in person."

Biggles smiled faintly. "I see. By the way, what's your name?"

"Cadet Corporal Masters, sir—Peter Masters."

"How old are you?"

"Nearly seventeen, sir."

"So you'll soon be coming into the service?"

"I hope so, sir."

Biggles pulled forward a scribbling pad. "Good. Now, what is this you want to discuss with me?"

"This morning, sir," began Peter, "when I was working on a machine in a hangar, I couldn't help overhearing a conversation between two officers. One of them was saying that he heard a German prisoner tell the interviewing officer that the Nazis have a huge petrol store in the Black Forest, where the British could never find it."

Biggles nodded. "Yes, I heard something about that. Go on."

"I've got an idea I know where that dump is, sir," declared Peter.

Biggles looked incredulous. "How on earth could you know that?"

"Because, unless I'm mistaken, I've actually seen it."

The Air Commodore was now all attention. "Pull up a chair; sit down and tell us all you know," he invited briskly. "Presumably you've been to Germany?"

"Yes, sir," answered Peter as he sat down. "I lived in Germany for eleven years. You see, my father was in the Diplomatic Service. We lived at Karlsruhe, but he was recalled on the outbreak of war."

"I see," said Biggles slowly, his eyes on Peter's face. "Go ahead."

"When I was in Germany," resumed Peter, "I often took long walks in the Black Forest. One day I went farther than usual, right up into the hills —farther than I should have gone, because the district was a game preserve that belonged to one of the head Nazis. For that reason I took care to keep among the trees, in case there were any game-keepers about. In a glade I was brought to a stop by a barbed wire fence; and beyond it, on the slope of a hill, was the last thing I expected to see there —I don't really know why. It was a poultry farm. At least, that's what it looked like. There were wooden sheds at regular intervals, with a few chickens pecking about, although not as many as you'd expect considering the number of huts." Peter paused.

"Go on," said Biggles quietly, after a glance at the Air Commodore.

"Well, sir, I had my dog with me," went on Peter. "He was only a pup, so he was not very obedient, and before I could stop him he was through the fence chasing one of the chickens. He chased it into one of the huts, where from the noise it made I thought he was killing it; so to save it I climbed the fence and rushed to the hut. I saved the bird and caught the pup. Then, looking round, it struck me that this was a queer sort of business. To start with there were no perches. Then I saw that the floor was of concrete, which seemed an awful waste of money—particularly as the Nazis don't usually throw money away. In the middle of the floor there was an iron manhole. I wasn't thinking of spying. I was too young then to understand such things, but I couldn't help wondering what could be under a henhouse. So I lifted the cover and looked in. There was nothing there. It just seemed to be an enormous empty reservoir. There were iron steps, but I didn't go down because I could hear men talking not far away. I fancy they were still working on the place. So I replaced the cover and bolted back the way I had come. That's all, sir."

"Didn't you tell your father about this?" asked the Air Commodore.

"No, sir," replied Peter. "At that time—it was in the summer of nineteen thirty-eight—the Nazis were getting very strict, and my father warned me constantly not to pry about, as it might get us all into trouble. I thought he'd be angry with me if he knew what I'd done, so I said nothing, and after a time I forgot all about the incident. In fact, I forgot all about it until this morning when I heard the officers talking about a secret dump. Then it struck me all of a heap, as they say, that the thing I had seen, the reservoir, might be a vast petrol storage tank. I can't think of any reason why the Nazis should put a water tank there."

The Air Commodore was leaning forward now, his eyes like gimlets. "You never saw this place again?"

"No, sir."

"Could you mark it on the map?"

"I don't think so, sir," admitted Peter frankly. "You see, the Black Forest is all very much alike— or that part of it was; mostly fir trees, with glades between. I should know the place again though, if I saw it."

"You couldn't give me precise directions for finding it?"

Peter shook his head. "No, sir. You see, I was only rambling, without paying much attention to where I was going. There were no roads, or even paths, that might serve as a guide. But I know the district so well that if I saw it again I could go straight to the spot."

"Do you think you could recognize the place from an aircraft?"

"Yes, sir. I'm pretty sure of it. Looking at an actual place is a lot easier than trying to mark it on a map."

The Air Commodore looked at Biggles meaningly. "I'd wager any money that what this lad saw was the petrol dump. I don't see how it can be anything else. The fact that there was a barbed wire fence round it to keep people away suggests that it was something secret, and important." Turning back to Peter he added: "How far were you from Karlsruhe when you saw this place?"

"About nine miles, in a south-east direction."

"Could a pilot find the place from that description?"

"I shouldn't think so, sir," answered Peter.

"Not if he spotted the henhouses?"

"No, because there are genuine poultry farms at no great distance, and unless the pilot knew the country as I do, the chances are that he would choose the wrong one."

The Air Commodore was silent for a minute or two. "Just one last question," he said slowly. "In an emergency, would you be prepared to fly over one night in one of our machines and help the pilot to find the place?"

Peter's eyes glowed. "Rather!" he said enthusiastically. "But it wouldn't be much use going at night, I'm afraid."

"Why not?"

"The Black Forest is black enough by day. It would be hopeless to look for the glade at night, even though the henhouses were still there. I could only promise to find it by day."

"Very well. Would you go by day?"

"Yes, sir."

"You'd have to get your father's permission."

"My father is dead, sir," answered Peter quietly. "He was killed at Dunkirk. I live with my aunt; her husband, my uncle, is now in the navy. I'm sure he wouldn't object to my going."

"I haven't said yet that you are going," murmured the Air Commodore drily. "But I may find it necessary to ask you. I'll let you know later. In the meantime, say nothing of this to anyone. You were quite right to report it; it may lead to bigger things than you imagine. That's all for now."

"Thank you, sir." Peter saluted and went out.

As the door closed behind him the Air Commodore turned to Biggles. There was a twinkle in his eyes, but his manner was alert. "I think we've got something here," he said tersely. "It looks like a job for you."

Biggles smiled. "I was afraid it might come to that. What do you want me to do—go over and have a look at the place?"

The Air Commodore shook his head. "No. If the Nazis see a British machine prowling about round the dump—if it is a dump—they'll guess we're on the track of something. The thing to do is to hit it, hit it hard, before they have a chance to do anything. The roof of that storage tank can't be very thick—two or three feet of concrete at most. A five hundred pound bomb would go through it like a bullet going through butter. If the petrol is there, that ought to settle it. If not—well, no great harm will have been done."

"Sounds like a job for a Mosquito."

"Just what I was thinking," agreed the Air Commodore. "But I doubt if one machine would be, enough. There is always a chance of a miss. I feel inclined to send a small compact formation to make sure. But before we discuss this any further, will you do the job? If so, I should be content to leave the organization of it to you. You can have what machines you like, and I'll help you in every way as far as is in my power."

"Yes, sir, of course I'll do it," consented Biggles. "Some of my boys are getting a bit restless now that we have to fly so far to find the Luftwaffe, and a show will do them good. But what about this lad, Cadet Masters? It rather looks as if everything depends on him. If what he says is true, and I don't doubt it, without him we might have a dickens of a job to find the target. Yet he's too young for regular enlistment."

The Air Commodore's eyes smiled. "Not necessarily. There are such things as special enlistments, and this seems to be a case where one is indicated. Leave it to me. I'll fix it up with the Inspector of Recruiting. You go ahead with your plans. By the time you are ready, Masters will be an airman serving on your station. Now I must be getting back to the Air Ministry. I'm glad I looked in."

The Air Commodore shook hands and departed.

Three days later the adjutant again put his head into the C.O.'s office.

"You wanted to see Aircraftman Masters when he reported for duty, sir. He's here now," he announced.

"Send him right in," answered Biggles. "Ask

Flight Lieutenants Lacy and Lissie, and Flying Officers Hebblethwaite and Carrington, to come along right away."

"Yes, sir."

Peter Masters, looking rather conscious of his brand new uniform, marched in and saluted.

"So you're in the service, eh?" smiled Biggles. "We're going to have a short conference, so you might as well sit down. I'm just waiting for the officers who are going on the show with us."

Presently they appeared—Flight Lieutenant "Algy" Lacey, quietly confident, Flight Lieutenant Lord Bertie Lissie, monocle in eye, looking slightly bored; Flying Officer "Ginger" Hebblethwaite, slightly dishevelled from playing squash, and Flying Officer "Tug" Carrington, as usual, grim and truculent. His parents had been killed in a London blitz.

"All right. Sit down, everybody." Biggles indicated Peter. "This is Masters, who is going to act as pathfinder for the sortie, which you all know about. I'm just going to run over the brief, so that everyone will know precisely what we have to do. In particular, I want you, Masters, to pay particular attention, bearing in mind that it is not too late to draw back if you think that the job is asking too much of you."

"No fear of that, sir," said Peter.

"That's the spirit," answered Biggles. "The raid has been timed to leave the ground at six o'clock to-morrow evening. I've chosen that time because a squadron of Lancasters is going to blast the Messerschmitt works at Augsburg, which is just beyond our objective, to-morrow evening, and we may help each other by splitting the enemy's fighter defences. We may not see anything of the Lancasters, but it doesn't matter. Our striking force will consist of three Mosquitos, each of which will carry a crew of two." Biggles looked at Peter. "Have you ever seen a Mosquito?"

"Yes, sir, often," replied Peter. "I have helped to clean them down."

"Good. Then there is no need for me to describe the machine," went on Biggles. "It's probably the best and fastest long-range medium bomber in the world, specially designed for daylight raids. I shall lead the show carrying four five-hundred pound bombs. You will act as my observer, and your job will be to take me over the target—we'll have a practice run or two presently. For your information, Peter, for low level work the observer rarely uses the prone position for bombing in, but you may do so if it will help you to find the target. Remember, the other two pilots will be behind us, and their observers will watch for hostile aircraft. The other two machines will be flown by Flight Lieutenants Lacey and Lissie, with Flying Officers Hebblethwaite and Carrington as observers. They will also carry four five-hundred pound high explosive bombs. The attack will be made from low level, in line astern, so all bombs will be fitted with delayed action fuses to ensure that we get clear before they explode. After bombing, the machines will break formation, but will get together again for the run home." Biggles paused to light a cigarette.

"On the principle that the shortest distance between two points is a straight line, I shall fly a direct compass course to the scene of operations. As we approach the target area, as I said just now, you, Peter, will take your place in the transparent nose, and guide me over this dummy hen farm. Try to get it at the first run if you can, because the longer we are about the job the more likely we are to get a plastering from the ground defences—if there are any. That's really all there is to it, except that Flight Lieutenant Lacey will carry a camera, so that when we get home we can observe at leisure the result of the raid. The six officers of the squadron who are not taking part in the actual sortie will come to meet us in Spitfires, to form an escort, should we need one, on the final section of the run home. They'd be doing a sweep over France anyway, so they may as well hold an umbrella over us in case it starts raining Messerschmitts. I think that's all. Has anyone any questions to ask?"

"It seems straightforward to me," remarked Algy.

"Absolutely," agreed Bertie, polishing his monocle.

"All right. In that case we'll have a look at the map, after which I'll give Masters a practice run or two in my Mosquito."

Ginger winked at Peter. "You're a lucky lad, getting on a show like this so soon."

"It's really his show," observed Biggles.

"I only hope those fake henhouses are still there," murmured Peter. "I shall feel a silly fool if they've gone."

The following afternoon, at ten minutes to six, walking awkwardly in his parachute harness Peter followed the officers to the tarmac where three Mosquitos stood in charge of a flight sergeant, with their twin engines ticking over like well-oiled sewing machines.

By this time Peter knew the routine fairly well, for he had made several practice flights with his

leader, using an old cottage as a target. He had
decided to use the prone position, lying flat to look
down through the transparent nose, only when they
approached the target area. He had also become
more or less accustomed to the rather terrifying
sensation of rushing along just above the surface of the
ground at several miles a minute. Standing by
Biggles, whom he had long admired, he wondered
for a moment if this could really be happening,
that he was about to take the air on a hazardous
operational flight with one of the best pilots in the
Royal Air Force. It seemed too good to be true.

He watched the rear part of the aircraft, containing
oxygen, the radio, recognition lights, and other
fixed equipment, sealed, as it always is before a
flight. No entry into this part of the machine is
possible during the operation. He then climbed
into his seat, which was on the right hand side of the
pilot. He thrilled with anticipation as the engines
were run up, and the bomb doors closed.

A minute later the aircraft was streaking across
the turf at unbelievable speed, its retractable undercarriage, and tail-wheel folding, as a bird's legs fold
into its body.

Sitting beside Biggles, for a while Peter gazed
fixedly through the windscreen at the curious spectacle
of the world rushing towards him. It was as though
the earth was spinning madly in the opposite direction.
A tall tree, or a high building, would appear on the
horizon, to hurtle, it seemed, towards the Mosquito.
Then it would flash past, to be seen no more. The
sensation of speed was terrific. He had flown before,
but never had he known anything like this. This
was *really* flying, flying at a speed no bird could equal.

Once he glanced half furtively at his pilot, the man whose hand and brain controlled this incredible vehicle, this veritable magic carpet. His face was expressionless. His eyes gazed steadily ahead through the windscreen. He appeared to be doing nothing, creating the impression that such flying was easy. This, Peter was aware, was a delusion. That small firm hand that rested on the control column was the connecting link between his brain and the immense power compressed into the two engines. Should it fail, even for a split second, the result would be fatal.

During one of the practice runs Peter had asked Biggles why it was necessary to fly at such tremendous speed, and Biggles had pointed out that the Mosquito was essentially a day bomber. Night bombers, he asserted, could carry an enormous load of bombs, but usually they had to operate at a high altitude, which meant that they could not single out a small individual target with guaranteed accuracy.

The coast appeared. In an instant land had given way to the cold green water of the Channel. To the Mosquito it was little more than a ditch. Magically another coast appeared, and Biggles pressed gently on the control column until the Mosquito appeared to be skimming the waves.

Peter wondered why Biggles flew so low, and asked the question.

Biggles answered: "The lower we fly, the harder it is to see us; consequently, by flying very low, we try to hold the element of surprise. That is to say, I hope to dash past the enemy guns before the gunners see us—or at any rate, before they can bring their guns to bear. On a sortie like this the correct landfall

H

is very important. If we had to fly up and down the coast looking for a landmark the enemy would have time to prepare a hot reception for us. All the same, we may see some fireworks. Are the other two machines behind us?"

Peter glanced over his shoulder. "Yes, sir, they're both with us."

"Good." Biggles' hand tightened on the control column, and the Mosquito flashed across the coast. An instant later lines of glittering tracer shells poured up from several places on the ground, but they all appeared to go behind the formation.

A ghost of a smile crossed Biggles' face. "Look over your head," he said.

Peter looked up, and caught his breath when he saw great clouds of black smoke. In the heart of each one, as it blossomed out against the blue sky, was an orange flame.

"That's a heavy anti-aircraft battery farther down the coast having a crack at us," said Biggles calmly. "They're using short-fused shells, but they can't get their guns low enough to hit us. Remember what I said about flying low?" Biggles tilted a wing-tip to miss a tall poplar tree. "Are the other two machines all right?"

Again Peter glanced behind, and saw the other Mosquitos tearing along slightly astern, and a little to one side of the leader. "Yes, sir, they're still with us," he answered, enthusiastically, as the spirit of the affair warmed his blood and set his pulses tingling.

There were no more shells. Instead, the long hedgeless fields of northern France, dotted with farmhouses, began to flash past. Peter saw men and women working in the fields, and realized with sorrow that they were slaves of the Nazis. The people looked up as they passed. Some waved; others held up their arms erect in the form of a letter V.

"They're giving us the victory sign!" cried Peter, suddenly understanding.

"They usually do," answered Biggles. "They're pleased to see us. Imagine how you would feel, if you were a slave down there in occupied country, and saw friends coming over to thrash the taskmasters. They can't speak to us, but that doesn't prevent them from letting us know how they feel. You'll see the people of Belgium doing it too, presently, when we cut across the south eastern tip, and the people of Luxembourg."

The Mosquito roared on, skimming the trees, sometimes even flashing between them, to tear across a pasture or field of corn, and jump the hedge at the far side. Peter began to understand why pilots called this sort of flying "hedge-hopping." It was like a glorified steeplechase, with an aeroplane for a mount instead of a horse.

Time passed. The three Mosquitos sped on, never more than a few feet apart. Once Peter saw a number of black specks in the sky far to the north, and he called his pilot's attention to them.

Biggles merely glanced at them and said: "Messerschmitt 109's."

"Will they catch us?" asked Peter.

"No," answered Biggles. "I doubt if they'll try, because they know we can show them our heels. If they were in front of us it would be different. As it is, they may sit upstairs and wait for us to come home."

The Messerschmitts fell farther and farther behind, and finally disappeared.

"That's the river Moselle we're just passing. Germany ahead," said Biggles. "We shall be over the Rhine in a minute or two. That should tell you just where we are. I shall aim to leave Karlsruhe just on my left. I'll warn you when we sight the city. That will be your cue to get down and give me a line on the hen roosts." Biggles smiled. "If there are any birds in that paddock I'm afraid they're going to have an awful shock. It will be their unlucky day."

"The Nazis will probably have eaten them by now," replied Peter.

"There you are, that's Karlsruhe on the left," said Biggles sharply. "I'm relying on you now; I'm still heading south-east, so get your bearings and tell me where you want me to go."

As Peter dropped to the floor Biggles gave the order to the other two machines. "Line astern."

With his nerves quivering now that the great moment had come Peter lay flat on his stomach and stared down through the transparent floor at the expanse of country that became wider as the Mosquito climbed. The reason for this climb when nearing the target, Biggles had explained, was to avoid the risk of being hit by one of their own bombs, should it bounce, as sometimes happened. With mixed feelings Peter picked out the path that he had taken with his pup on the day that he had discovered the strange poultry farm. So much had happened since, it seemed as if he had lived a lifetime. Flushed with excitement, now that everything depended on him, his eyes followed the path to where it disappeared beneath the sombre firs that clad the rolling hillside. To his infinite relief nothing appeared to have changed. The henhouses were just beyond the second ridge, a little to the left.

"Left—left!" he called sharply.

The nose of the aircraft came round a trifle, but not quite enough.

"Left—left!" he cried again.

The nose of the aircraft moved, a trifle too much, as it flashed across the first ridge.

"Right—right!" called Peter in a clear voice.

The nose moved again.

"Steady!"

The Mosquito flashed across the second ridge, and there before Peter's eyes, perhaps half a mile ahead, lay the innocent target. The henhouses were still there. No fowls could be seen, but a man who was walking across the open ground stopped suddenly, stared for a moment at the approaching aircraft, and then made a dash for the timber that fringed the boundary.

"There they are! There are the hen-sheds," rapped out Peter. "You can see them for yourself now. I should aim for the middle." He felt rather than saw the bomb doors open.

By the time he had finished speaking the Mosquito was almost over the wire boundary fence. Up to this point nothing had happened. The sylvan scene might well have been all that it pretended to be. Then, in an instant of time, it changed. Short jabbing yellow flames appeared at several points, and lines of white fire streamed upwards, converging on the aircraft. Peter knew well enough that these were tracer shells, and the fact that the place was defended at once confirmed his suspicions. Had there been nothing to defend, there would be no anti-aircraft guns. He flinched as an explosion rocked the machine, and made the fabric quiver like the hide of a startled horse.

But the shooting did not remain all one way. The nose of the Mosquito tilted downward, and the four cannon, and four machine guns with which it was fitted, poured out a hail of metal. This state of affairs lasted only for two seconds. The aircraft seemed to jump an invisible object as its bombs hurtled downwards; then it screamed into the air like a rocket, at the same time turning away in a vertical bank.

Peter caught a fleeting glimpse of the two other Mosquitos roaring skyward; then he got back into his seat beside the pilot—not without difficulty, for centrifugal force seemed to clamp him to the floor. He looked down. The air was still full of flying tracer bullets, but as far as he could make out nothing had happened. The glade looked just the same. A wave of bitter disappointment surged over him. Had they come all this way for nothing? He snatched a glance at Biggles. The pilot was also looking down. His face was expressionless.

Then Peter remembered that the bombs carried delayed action fuses. He looked down again at the glade, now falling away astern; and as he watched, pillars of flame shot into the air from several points. Just what happened after that was not easy to see. The flames seemed to meet, and then leap higher. The glade became a roaring inferno, erupting fire and smoke. It was the smoke that fascinated Peter, black, oily smoke that twisted and turned upon itself in a vast coiling column that went up and up until it seemed to touch the dome of heaven—a fearful, awe-inspiring spectacle. A Mosquito came tearing past it like a fly dodging a cauldron, and he guessed that it was the machine that had been detailed to get the photographs.

Peter felt a touch on his arm, and looked up to see Biggles smiling faintly.

"You were right, laddie," said Biggles. "There must have been a million gallons of oil in that dump. Judging by the way it went up I'd say there were two dumps—oil and petrol. We got them both. The Nazis will see that pillar of smoke for a hundred miles."

"And now what do we do?" asked Peter.

Biggles' eye twinkled. "We get home just as fast as we can."

As far as Peter could see this presented no difficulty. The flight, he thought, had passed its climax. In this he was wrong. With more experience he was to learn that the bombing of a target in daylight is an incident marking the beginning of the real peril. It marks the position of the aircraft beyond all shadow of doubt, and the information is flashed throughout enemy territory, with the result that all arms, both in the air and on the ground, are brought to bear, to prevent the raiders from getting home.

Very soon Peter sensed this from his pilot's manner; far from relaxing, Biggles seemed to stiffen. His eyes were never still. They roved the air incessantly, above and around. Once, in a brittle voice, he told the other two machines to close up. Then, as if they were united by invisible wires, the three Mosquitos sped across the landscape at an altitude never more than a hundred feet.

Peter did not see the first enemy aircraft arrive. The first indication he had of it was the grunting of its guns and the sight of tracer bullets streaming across their nose. Something struck the Mosquito near the tail with a crack like a whiplash. Biggles had evidently seen the machine, for he said, without emotion, for Peter's benefit: "Focke-Wulf 190."

"Are we going to attack it?" asked Peter.

"No, worse luck," answered Biggles. "We're too far from home. If we started fooling about here it would give every fighter in the Luftwaffe a chance to catch up with us, and we should soon have a pack of wolves to deal with. We've got to get home—at least, that's the idea."

Then began a curious running fight, with the three Mosquitos racing just above the ground, taking evasive action all the time, with the Focke-Wulf in pursuit. It lasted for about five minutes, with the Nazi machine falling farther and farther behind. The pilot seemed to be troubled by the trees between which the Mosquitos often flashed; at any rate, he refused to take such risks, with the result that he lost ground by going round them.

Biggles glanced in the reflector and smiled. "The Nazi pilots are not very good at hedge-hopping," he remarked. "Last week I saw one try it, but he finished up in some telegraph wires. He made an awful mess of himself—and the wires." Biggles laughed at the recollection. Then he became serious. "Hello! What's this coming?"

Peter snatched a glance upwards and saw a swarm

An instant later a Messerschmidt, upside down, went past so close that Peter flinched.

His mouth went dry with shock.

of Messerschmitts dropping like vultures out of the sky.

Biggles did not alter his course, but he kept his eyes on the enemy aircraft. "Eighteen of them," he muttered. "They'll probably get in each other's way."

Of the next five minutes Peter had only a hazy recollection. He saw a machine carrying the swastika device shoot across their bows, swing up in a steep climbing turn, and then come down at them, guns spitting. Biggles lifted the Mosquito's nose a trifle. Tracer flashed, and the enemy machine seemed to go to pieces in the air. An instant later a Messerschmitt, upside-down, went past so close that Peter flinched. His mouth went dry with shock.

"I fancy Algy must have got that one," murmured Biggles dispassionately.

As things turned out Biggles was right about the Messerschmitts getting in each other's way. Several machines came tearing towards the leading Mosquito. Biggles turned in a flash. The Messerschmitts tried to follow, but they were too close to each other and had to open out to avoid collision. As it was, the wings of two of them became locked, and they plunged earthward. Then somehow, the sky ahead was clear.

"Are the others still with us?" asked Biggles calmly.

Peter looked back. He moistened his lips. "Yes, they're still there."

"Fine," murmured Biggles. "I think we can say good-bye to those Messerschmitts."

The Mosquitos roared on. Biggles resumed his systematic scrutiny of the sky, pulling down dark glasses for the purpose. Peter did the same, for the setting sun was now directly in their eyes, making it difficult to see straight ahead without suffering temporary blindness.

For some time nothing happened, then Biggles leaned forward. "Looks like another spot of trouble ahead," said he.

Peter had seen nothing, and it worried him that his pilot should always be the first to see everything. It was uncanny, the way Biggles seemed to miss nothing. It was, he concluded—correctly, of course— the result of experience. He had still much to learn.

It was Biggles, too, who announced the identity of the machines. "It's the Lancasters, on the way home after bombing Augsburg," he said tersely. "One—two—three . . . only nine of them. That means they've lost three. Pity—but that's not bad, considering where they've been. I'm afraid they're still having a rough time, too."

As the three Mosquitos overtook the Lancasters Peter got a clear view of the picture. It was obvious that a deadly combat was raging. The nine Lancasters were in a tight formation, wing tip to wing tip, on a straight course for home at about a thousand feet. Around them, wheeling and zooming and shooting, and diving to shoot again, was a mixed crowd of enemy aircraft, mostly Messerschmitts and Focke-Wulfs. Peter reckoned that there were not fewer than twenty of them. These were not having things all their own way, for streams of tracer bullets pouring from the gun turrets of the Lancasters revealed that most of the gunners were still in action. Even as Peter watched, a Messerschmitt suddenly spurted a plume of black smoke; an instant later a tongue of flame leapt from its engine and licked hungrily towards the tail. The nose of the stricken Messerschmitt tilted downward in a dive that became ever steeper. A figure detached itself and dropped like a stone.

Peter glanced at Biggles and saw that his lips were set in a thin, bloodless line. "What are we going to do?" he asked.

"Our job is to get home," answered Biggles in a hard voice. "We're much faster than the Lancasters so we can't stay with them." A ghost of a smile played for a moment about his lips. "All the same, I don't see why we shouldn't give our lads a spot of encouragement as we go past." Then he spoke into the radio.

"Tallyho! Tallyho! Line abreast—line abreast. I'm going up to scatter the Huns, but carry straight on. Here we go—here we go." To Peter Biggles said: "Hold your breath."

As far as Peter was concerned this admonition was really unnecessary. As the nose of the Mosquito went down for maximum speed, and zoomed up like a rocket, he held his breath—or rather, he forgot to breathe. The combat seemed to float towards them, and he braced his muscles for the collision that seemed inevitable. At the back of his mind a conviction was born that this was not really happening, that it was a dream.

The Mosquito passed so close to the rear Lancaster that he distinctly saw the tail gunner's face as he crouched behind his guns. He was smiling, which struck Peter as strange. He couldn't see what there was to laugh at. It was all too terrifying. To start with, the wings of the other Mosquitos, one on either side of them, seemed to be touching their own. That alone was alarming enough; but it was nothing to what was to come.

Like sharks darting into a school of small fish the Mosquitos flashed into the combat. In a moment all position was lost on both sides. Tracer shells and bullets flashed. Aircraft swerved, dived, and zoomed. Swastikas were everywhere. A Focke-Wulf, wrapped in a sheet of flame, tore past the nose of Biggles' Mosquito, the pilot leaping into space even as it passed. Peter saw every detail of the machine distinctly, and the picture remained engraved on his brain. Just beyond, two Messerschmitts, one minus a wing, were spinning earthward together. Something smote the Mosquito like a flail, and Peter clutched wildly at the side of the machine as Biggles zoomed vertically. White pencil lines of tracer bullets were everywhere, like tiny comets. After that, all Peter saw was sky, with occasinal machines outlined against it. Once he saw the Lancasters, still in formation, at a curious angle. Then, in some miraculous way Biggles' Mosquito was racing along on even keel just above the ground, with the other two Mosquitos closing in on it. Subconsciously he noted that Algy's machine had lost a wing tip. There were holes all along the fuselage.

Peter shook his head. He seemed to be having difficulty in thinking clearly. He could not make up his mind whether his brain was working slowly, or if things were happening faster than his brain could follow. He looked at Biggles, and saw that he was sitting in his seat, just the same as usual. As far as he was concerned the combat might not have happened. He looked to the right and saw Bertie Lissie. His monocle was still in his eye. Bertie looked across and made a funny face. Peter began to wonder what sort of men these were who could make a joke of death—or at any rate, treat fear as if it did not exist.

Looking about him he made out the Lancasters about a mile behind, and a fair distance above them. It seemed that Biggles' charge had served a useful purpose, for there were fewer enemy aircraft than there had been, and those that remained were some distance away, hanging on the flanks of the British machines rather than pressing home their attack. He looked down at the ground and observed that they were now over the unmistakable fields of northern France.

Biggles evidently divined his thoughts, for he said: "We're getting near the Channel." He looked at Peter's face. "How do you feel?"

Peter moistened his lips, which were still dry. "Not bad."

Biggles nodded. "That's the spirit. That was rather a hot minute, for a chap on his first sortie. You get used to it after a time."

That, judging from Biggles' manner, was true, but all the same, Peter found himself wondering what sort of nerves were possessed by these men who could go on doing this sort of thing, flirting with Old Man Death, day in and day out, for months at a stretch. What amazed him most was their coolness. Were they so cold-blooded that they could never get excited? Nothing seemed to disturb their equanimity. Would he, he wondered, ever reach that degree of calm efficiency? He could only hope so.

Biggles spoke again. "There's the Channel," he announced.

"Then we're nearly home," cried Peter.

"Nearly—but not quite," murmured Biggles.

"There's a crowd of Huns coming up from the south. They've spotted us, and I fancy they're not feeling at all friendly."

"How do you know they've spotted us?" asked Peter.

"I saw them change course towards us a moment ago," answered Biggles.

Peter looked at the unruffled, clean-shaven face of the man who seemed to see everything. He found it a queer sensation to reflect that within the next few minutes he would either be safe, on his own aerodrome, or dead. One of the two things would happen. Biggles must realize that, too, he thought, although he showed no sign of it. Or had he become so used to it that he didn't even think about it? That, he suspected, was the answer.

Biggles interrupted his reverie. "Here they come," he said, nodding towards a cluster of specks that were streaming down from a great height to cut them off. "Hold your hat. If they get in my way I'm going right through them."

"Wouldn't it be better to try to dodge them?" suggested Peter, a trifle anxiously.

Biggles gave him a reproachful look. "In the Royal Air Force we don't turn for Nazis—or anyone else. It isn't done. We make them turn. They know it, and perhaps that's why they usually get out of the way. Never forget that."

"Suppose one doesn't turn, one day?" inquired Peter, curiously.

Biggles smiled. "In that case it's going to be just too bad for everybody." He took a firmer grip on the control column, and spoke over the radio to Algy and Bertie. "Tallyho, boys. Don't let 'em get in your way. We're going straight home. The coffee will be getting cold."

As Biggles finished speaking he pushed the control column forward and sent a stream of bullets at some aircraft that were lined up in front of a bomb-blasted hangar. Peter hadn't noticed the enemy aerodrome. He felt the sensation of personal satisfaction that is the privilege of an air fighter, when he saw a number of Nazi airmen, who presumably had been working on the machines, run like hares for cover. Not all of them reached it. Some fell, and lay where they had fallen.

"That must have surprised them," remarked Peter.

"I hope so," replied Biggles evenly. "In the early days of the war they were fond of doing that sort of thing to helpless civilians, including women and children. There is, as you see, such a thing as poetic justice."

Biggles said no more, but turned his attention to the hostile machines that were now closing in on the three Mosquitos. Peter did not need telling that this last onset was going to be serious. Aircraft were dotted all over the sky—Messerschmitts, Heinkels and Folke-Wulfs. He formed the opinion that the approach of the Mosquitos had been signalled, with the result that all available Nazi machines had been sent into the air to form a cordon.

"This is going to be sticky," said Peter.

"It is, but perhaps not the way you think," returned Biggles.

"What do you mean?" asked Peter quickly.

"Keep your eyes open and you may see something."

Peter glanced at his companion. "I don't understand. The enemy seems to have us in a trap."

"Maybe the enemy is in a trap," replied Biggles vaguely. "When the Germans are cocksure of something they are apt to behave foolishly. Those fellows have been silly to split up like that, instead of keeping in formation. As a matter of fact, I'm not sorry to see them."

"Not sorry?"

"The anti-aircraft guns won't dare to put up a barrage for fear of hitting their own men. Well, here we go."

The enemy planes were now pouring down to the attack. Biggles was still roaring along at roof level. Peter watched him, realizing that he was with a master pilot and hoping to learn something from his tactics. He did, but it was hardly what he expected. Just what happened he did not see, because his head was suddenly jammed against the head rest by a frightful pressure that made everything go blurred and dim before his eyes. When he could see properly they were on a new course, at right angles to the original one. In some amazing way the other two Mosquitos had remained with their leader, but the enemy machines were some distance behind. Foiled for the moment, they at once resumed the pursuit.

"They're coming after us," announced Peter.

Biggles winked. "You watch them change their minds in a minute."

"Why should they change their minds?"

"Look up beyond the Messerschmitts."

Peter looked. At first he could not see anything because of the glare; then he made out a group of specks, looking rather like flies over a garden path on a summer evening. They grew rapidly larger. Then, suddenly, he understood. "They're Spitfires!" he cried.

"Quite right," agreed Biggles. "Some of the boys have come to meet us. I told them we should be along about this time."

"Then why did you turn as you did?" asked Peter.

"To upset the enemy," answered Biggles. "I wanted the Nazis to keep their eyes on us, so that they did not notice the Spitfires coming along above them. My new course took them right under the Spitfires."

"You saw the Spitfires then?" ejaculated Peter.

"Of course," answered Biggles evenly. "You have to keep your eyes open at this game."

Peter asked no more questions. He was too interested in watching what was happening behind them. What Biggles had predicted came true. The enemy planes abandoned their pursuit of the Mosquitos as they were compelled to turn to defend themselves. From being attackers they became the attacked, and the swift change-over appeared to throw them into confusion. The Spitfires, with the advantage of height, hurtled down on them, guns streaming cannon shells and bullets. Two Messerschmitts crumpled under the first devastating blast. Another burst into flames and went down in a series of stalling turns. Another spun viciously. Fascinated, Peter watched it go down until with a mighty splash it struck the sea. He had not realized that they had crossed the coast. It was hard to see what had happened after that, because the Mosquitos raced on, and the dog-fight was soon lost in the distance. He was worried for the Spitfires' pilots.

"Will our chaps be all right?" he asked.

"Probably," answered Biggles.

"Shouldn't we wait for them?"

"In modern flying," answered Biggles, "the great thing is to do that you are told. We were briefed to bomb a target and then come home. That's what we've done. The Spits were sent out to escort us over the last part of the journey, and that's what they're doing. They'll follow us home."

Peter sat back in his seat, feeling curiously limp from reaction now that the strain had relaxed. He realized that although unaware of it his nerves had been at full stretch. Yet, during the Battle of Britain, he reflected, British pilots had flown and fought against overwhelming odds, not once, but four, five, and even six times a day, for weeks on end. In the light of his recent experience the victory they had won now appeared in the nature of a miracle. Dusk was closing in as Peter watched the rolling English fields draw near. He saw the aerodrome emerge from the darkening landscape, and, as in a dream, watched his pilot operate the mechanism that lowered the undercarriage. Biggles was whistling quietly to himself.

The aircraft landed as lightly as a bird; the wheels touched the turf, and ran on for a little way, so that the Mosquito came to a standstill in front of station headquarters. Mechanics ran out.

"Well, here we are," announced Biggles casually, and waved a greeting to the crews of the two other Mosquitos as they pulled up in a line. Then he dropped lightly to the ground.

Peter followed, to discover that his legs were strangely weak, and his limbs stiff. As the crews foregathered

Air Commodore Raymond came out to meet them.

"How did it go?" he asked.

"Quite nicely," answered Biggles. "The boy was quite right. The stuff was there. We made a sizeable bonfire of it."

"Have any trouble?" inquired the Air Commodore.

"Nothing to speak of," returned Biggles easily.

"No trouble at all," murmured Bertie Lissie, polishing his eyeglass.

The Air Commodore turned to Peter and held out his hand. "Congratulations," he complimented. "How did you enjoy your first show?"

"It was—er—terrific," stammered Peter, as they all walked towards headquarters.

He was wondering what, in Biggles' estimation, a *difficult* show would be like.

STORY
4

THE CHANCE OF A LIFETIME

A Story Of U-boat Warfare

I T is bad luck to be only seventeen years old when there is a war on. At sixteen a fellow knows that he is too young for serious fighting. At eighteen he may join the forces. But seventeen is neither one thing nor the other—an infuriating age. At least, Jack Carrington found it so. Of course, he had tried to enlist, in the R.A.F., the Navy, and the Army, in turn, but each time the recruiting sergeant had smiled and said that he must wait a little longer. True, he was in the local Sea Cadets, but that wasn't the same thing.

Another irritation was the fact that he appeared to live at the one place on the globe that was out of the war—the island of Trinidad, in the British West Indies, where his father was an engineer at the petroleum works. Admittedly, there had been rumours of U-boats, but he had never seen one. Nor, as far as he knew, had any of the pilots of the Fleet Air Arm flying-boat unit that had been sent to the island to protect the oil industry. Ships had been sunk; indeed, of late ships trading with the island had disappeared with increasing frequency, which certainly suggested that U-boats were not far away. But they were singularly elusive, and neither the naval patrols or air scouts could get a glimpse of them.

As the senior petty officer of the Cadet Corps, who knew the lie of the land intimately, he had once been given a flight in an operational flying-boat. It had lasted for six hours, and all he had seen, except for an occasional submarine chaser patrol, was the sea. Once the novelty of flying had worn off it had been rather a dull affair. The most interesting thing had been the pilot's description of how the anti-U-boat air patrols worked. The pilot's name was "Tiny" Hale—a grand chap. The other officers called him Tiny because he was the very reverse, standing over six feet in his socks.

Submarine spotting from the air, he learned, was quite an art, demanding infinite patience. All sorts of things float on the surface of the sea in war time, and the patrolling pilot had to investigate everything. The chances were usually in favour of the submarine commander, who proceeded with his decks awash, ready for instant diving the moment an aircraft appeared above the horizon. In a minute he could be a hundred feet under the water, heading in any direction, leaving the air pilot to guess his position. The expert hunter then had only one thing to look for—oil. The submarine commander was well aware of this, and took every precaution to prevent the escape of this significant clue.

Jack learned that the propeller shafts of the U-boats were fitted with special self-sealing devices. Exhausts closed automatically when the submarine dived. Nevertheless, explained Tiny, there might be a small amount of oil on the upper works of the ship; oil

138

might cling to the outside of the exhausts, or it could rise from a strained plate if the submarine had been damaged by a depth charge, or had bruised itself on the bottom. It only needed a few spots of oil to leave the tell-tale mark on the surface. The oil spots spread out, and when the sea was calm, could be seen from a great distance. So the pilot sat aloft, like a cat watching for a mouse, waiting for an oil trail to appear. On that particular day they had hunted for hours without seeing anything remotely resembling an oil trail.

Anyway, as far as Jack was concerned this was not war, and he fretted for the day when he would be able to take his place with his older friends in the battle line. Wherefore his lithe young figure drooped despondently; his clean-cut, sun-bronzed face was sad, and his clear blue eyes cloudy. He pushed his long fair hair from his forehead with an impatient gesture. Even his beloved sports of sailing, and exploring the neighbouring uninhabited islands, were beginning to pall, and he went out in his little skiff more from habit than any other reason. The skiff was fitted with a small outboard motor, but he seldom used it, regarding it rather as an emergency device in case of a dead calm.

As he walked along the white coral sand beach of such an island, a favourite haunt named Porpoise Island, on which he had landed to collect a few of the magnificent coconuts that grew there, he tried to console himself with the knowledge that it was at least a perfect day for sailing, even for a climate where the weather is always near perfection. Overhead the sun shone serenely from an unclouded sky of azure blue, while a light breeze rustled the palm fronds, and set little wavelets dancing on the trans-parent water—water so clear that from the skiff he could look through ten fathoms of it to the coral-strewn bed of the ocean.

He knew every inch of the island, for many and romantic were the legends connected with it. Chief of these was the usual pirate hoard. Some old in-habitants said that the treasure was buried on the island; others declared that it was in the hold of a galleon that had foundered while at anchor hard by the island, while the crew were getting fresh water. Naturally, such fascinating stories were not to be ignored, and Jack had searched every jungle-clad slope, every rock on the island, and in the water round it; but while he had found many strange things, gold and jewels were not among them. Still, he had not given up the search. He preferred to think that the treasure *might* be there. As he walked on, once he paused and threw a precautionary glance behind him to make sure that he had pulled the skiff high and dry, out of reach of wave and blistering sun. With his hands in the pockets of his canvas slacks, the only garment that he wore, he strolled on to the cove where the best nuts grew.

He had nearly reached the spot when footmarks in the sand brought him to a sudden halt. He was not alarmed; as far as he knew there was no reason why he should be; but he was surprised, because although he had made numerous visits to Porpoise Island he had never seen anyone there. Yet someone had obviously been there, and recently. Walking on, more slowly now, his brow darkened with anger when he saw that half a dozen fine trees, in the prime of life, had been felled, apparently as the easiest way

140

of obtaining the nuts that grew in the crowns. At any rate, the nuts had been taken. So, curiously enough, had some of the fronds. Wondering what sort of man could be such a fool, such a scoundrel, as to wantonly destroy trees that had taken many years to grow, he surveyed the scene, half expecting to see a ship. Not a speck broke the rippling surface. Then a possible explanation struck him. Perhaps some shipwrecked mariners, sailors from a torpedoed vessel, had managed to reach the island. If they were starving, and unable to get up to the nuts, then the vandalism might be pardoned. Evidently the men, whoever they were, had gone, unless they had transferred themselves to the far side of the island. His curiosity prompted him to find out.

It was a good way round the curving coastline, so to save time he decided to climb the central hill, and survey the far side of the island from its crest. As he knew every track made by the wild goats, this presented no difficulty.

As he climbed the hill, at a point beyond which the crags dropped sheer into a tiny cove, he became aware of something unusual. Something seemed to be missing. At first he could not make out what it was. Then he remembered. The sea birds. The gulls that nested on the island always seemed to resent his intrusion; they always followed him, uttering their harsh yet plaintive cries. Why were they not there? Then, listening, he heard them. The discordant chorus came from somewhere ahead, and the conclusion he reached was a natural one. The men who had cut down the palms were still on the island, and the gulls were devoting their attentions to them. His interest increased as he hurried on. Not for a moment did it occur to him that he stood in the slightest danger.

Yet when he had nearly reached the top of the hill that overlooked the cove, he dropped on his hands and knees, and went forward more cautiously. This was not prompted by fear. It was merely that he felt a natural disinclination to be caught spying on other people. At least, that was what other people might think. Actually, they had as much right on the island as he had, and it was not his place to interfere. He decided therefore, to see, without being seen, if this were possible.

The first thing he saw, when he peered between the rocks that littered the crest of the hill, was the seagulls. They were circling low over what appeared to be a long mass of debris, chiefly palm fronds. Every now and then one of the birds would swoop low and snatch something from the surface of the water. All of which struck Jack as mighty curious. The birds had never behaved like that before, and he knew enough of wild life to realize that such things usually have a meaning. Nor could he understand how such a mass of debris could have accumulated. If a current ran into the cove, surely the same thing would have happened before. He was sure it had not, or he would have noticed it. Presently, he wondered why he did not guess the truth instantly.

He was still lying on the hill, pondering this knotty problem, when it was answered for him. Two men, in thick trousers and heavy woollen sweaters, appeared out of the debris. They walked to a pile of loose rock, and pushing some of it aside, pulled out a pipe. This they started to drag towards the debris.

It was not until one of the men shouted something

that the first glimmerings of truth penetrated into Jack's brain. The language used was not English. It was German. He knew that well enough because he had so often heard it on the radio. When, a moment later, an engine started running somewhere under the accumulation of palm fronds, there was no longer any doubt. He realized that the heap of rubbish hid a submarine—a German submarine. It was now in process of taking in oil, or petrol, from a hidden supply tank. The island was, in fact, a secret U-boat refuelling station.

It is not to be supposed that this information merely floated into Jack's brain, leaving it undisturbed. Rather did it hit him in a series of shocks, shocks that left him strangely weak. As his excitement rose, his hands began to tremble, and his breathing became faster. What a discovery! He forgot the weather; forgot the original object of his visit to the island; he forgot everything, except the one stupendous fact that here, right under his nose, at a British island, was a German U-boat, quietly taking in stores. It can be no matter for wonder that it took him the best part of five minutes to recover his composure sufficiently to enable him to think coherently. The whole world seemed to have changed in a few moments. All other events faded into insignificance.

Once he recovered from the first stunning shock it did not take him long to decide on a course of action. He knew all that there was to know, and his obvious duty was to get the information, in the shortest possible space of time, to the Fleet Air Arm Commandant, who would know how to use it. Porpoise Island was nearly twenty miles from the depot, but that did not trouble him unduly. With a fair wind, and his little motor to help him, he should, he thought, be able to cover the distance in three hours. He did not know how long the U-boat had been there, but as far as he could make out it showed no signs of leaving.

With nerves tingling he backed away from the crest of the hill, and was about to rise to his feet, when a voice quite close to him said: "*Ach so!*"

The words, spoken in German, were almost like a blow, and he whirled round to find himself face to face with a heavily built sailor in German uniform.

The Nazi took a swift pace forward to seize him; but he was not fast enough. Jack twisted like an eel, and dashed off at an angle to the cover of some rocks. Unfortunately, the sailor had been standing in the one track that led down the hill, so his line of retreat to the place where he had left the skiff was for the moment cut off. He heard the German shout in a voice shrill with alarm. Answering shouts came from the cove, and Jack realized with a sinking feeling in the stomach that the worst possible thing had happened. He had stirred up a hornet's nest. The island would be combed for him by armed men, and unless he got away at once escape in the skiff would be impossible. The Germans would realize that he must have arrived in a boat of some sort, and they would do their utmost to prevent him from reaching it.

For a moment he crouched behind the rocks, his brain racing as never before. Then he broke cover and made a dash along the crest of the hill, hoping to reach another way down to the sea. If he could once gain the thick jungle that covered the lower slopes, he would be fairly safe, he thought. His intimate

144

knowledge of the terrain would give him an advantage over his pursuers.

But this was not to be. Before he had taken a dozen paces he saw another Nazi in front of him—this one armed with a rifle. The German saw him instantly, threw up the weapon and fired. The bullet missed, but it came uncomfortably close, and Jack knew that his life hung by a thread. If the Germans caught him they would kill him without mercy, knowing that he knew their secret.

Dodging and darting between rocks he sped on. Occasional shots smacking around him spurred him to desperate efforts. But these it seemed, were in vain, for Germans were now running from several directions, and some had gained the higher ground, from which they could command a view down the slope.

Unarmed, there was little he could do, and his common sense told him that it could only be a question of time before he was hit by a bullet. Several times he tried to creep down the slope without being seen, but on every occasion he came to an open space, to cross which would have been suicidal. He did not particularly mind being killed; what he could not bear was the thought of his knowledge dying with him. Each succeeding minute saw his position getting worse, for the Germans, knowing that he was still on the hill, were throwing a cordon round it to cut him off. Slowly but surely the net was tightened, forcing him back, until at last he lay flat among some rocks that lay strewn on the top of a small promontory. He could retreat no farther, for behind him the land ended abruptly in a cliff that dropped sheer for fifty feet into the ocean. With grim humour he perceived that he was, literally, between the devil and the deep blue sea. He could hear the Nazis coming, calling to each other as they advanced, and the sound nearly drove him frantic.

At that terrible moment it seemed that he had only one chance—a slim one, but still a chance. The Nazis would shoot him on sight. They had already made that abundantly clear. One course only was open. The sea. Having lived all his life on an island, he was, of course, nearly as much at home in the water as on land. He had dived high, but never from fifty feet. It looked a terrifying drop. But there was no other way. The Nazis would hardly dare to follow him, and there was just a chance that he might find a ledge, a crevice, at the base of the cliff, on which to rest, and hide, until darkness fell, when he might get away by swimming. At any rate, he decided, he would deny the Nazis the pleasure of shooting him.

Heavy footsteps crunching on the loose rock close at hand warned him that his time was short. He was about ten paces from the edge of the cliff, and he was aware that the moment he stood up he would be seen, in which case shots would be fired at him. That was a risk he would have to take. He derived a crumb of comfort from the knowledge that a fast moving target is not easy to hit with a rifle.

For a moment longer he lingered, tensing his muscles for the dash, drawing his legs under him in the manner of a runner getting into position for a sprint. Then he leapt to his feet and sped like an arrow for the void. There was a shout. Some shots were fired. One came close enough to snatch at his slacks. Then he was at the brink. There could have been no hesitation even if he had wished, for his impetus

146

carried him on. Like a bird he launched himself into space in a clean swallow dive, and the blue water seemed to rush up to embrace him.

Strangely enough, his brain was working with the smooth precision of a well-oiled piece of machinery. Not for a moment did he stop thinking, not even at the moment of impact, or when the water closed over him and he found himself in a profound blue world, lighted, it seemed, by turquoise floodlights overhead. As he turned towards the sombre shadow of the cliff he saw little shoals of fish darting away, and bubbles, like strings of pearls, rising from his body. Still under water he struck out for the cliff, hoping that there would be a certain amount of overhang which would prevent him from being seen by his enemies when his head broke the surface. If he did not reappear they might think that he had been drowned, or killed, perhaps, by one of the bullets that had been fired at the moment of his dive. That was what he hoped.

A small area of cliff, darker than the rest, attracted his attention. At first he took it to be a ledge that started somewhere in the depths, and ended a few inches above water level; and it was not until he reached out for it that he realized that far from being a shelf of rock, it was the reverse. There was nothing there. It was a cave. More than that he could not for the moment see. Nor was he particularly concerned, for his lungs were bursting. Come what may he had to breathe. Cautiously he raised his head above water, gulped a deep breath, and then took stock of his surroundings.

Except in one direction, the direction of the open water, all he could see was rock, for he was just inside a cave. It was not a cave in the true sense of the word, because nine tenths of it was under water. Between the smooth surface of the water and the roof of the cave was not more than eighteen inches, and it was into this small zone of air that he had stuck his head. It was ample for his purpose. In fact, he could not have wished for anything better. Very faintly he could hear the Nazis talking far above him.

Well satisfied with his find he turned to explore it, and perceived that it ran in for some way. Yet, curiously, it was not dark. A strange green light seemed to filter in from somewhere. Then he saw that he was in one of several caves, a veritable honeycomb of them, just at water level. Evidently there was a fault in the rock at that particular place, and the action of the waves had resulted in the caves— a by no means uncommon feature along rock-bound coasts. Without any particular object in view he floated farther into the cave, and discovered that the roof rose sharply until presently he was in a cave in the true meaning of the word. But it was such a cave that he could not have imagined. As he climbed ashore on a broad shelf of coral rock, the beauty of it took his breath away. Everything was green, glowing, luminous green. He had heard of the famous Blue Grotto at Capri, and supposed that this was a similar phenomenon. The water was like green fire. The drops that fell from his legs were sparkling emeralds.

At any other time he would have given himself up to contemplation of this delightful scene; but as things were, other matters weighed heavily on his mind. He had escaped from the Nazis, at any rate for the time being, but he still had to get home. For

148

the moment, of course, he could do nothing. No doubt the Germans were still about, and to show himself would be foolish. After dark it would be different. He ought to be able to slip away unseen.

Pulling himself a little higher on the coral ledge he found a keg. It was empty, but it told him that he was not the first visitor to this subterranean fairyland. The pirates must have known about this place, he conjectured, and used it as a hideout.

At this juncture he noticed that it was not quite as light as it had been, and it did not take him long to discover the reason. The water was rising, and the narrow channel of air was closing. He remembered that the tide was flooding, so there was nothing remarkable about this. Nor did it really matter, for he was not more than twenty feet from the open sea, and even though the cave became entirely submerged he could easily swim that distance.

Soon afterwards he realized that the tide had been a good friend to him. Strange sounds penetrated into his retreat; these, a movement of the water, and a sudden cutting off of the light that filtered in, could have only one explanation. A boat was passing the underwater entrance to the cave. The Nazis must have launched a dinghy, and were presumably looking for his body. Fortunately, the entrance to the cave was now entirely submerged, so they were hardly likely to find it. The light returned, and the water settled, suggesting that the boat had passed on. Jack settled himself on his ledge to wait for darkness.

It was a long wait, for it had been early afternoon when he had made his momentous discovery. But there was nothing else for it, and he whiled away

K

the time by exploring the cave, without discovering anything of note. Still, it was a fascinating place, and he decided that he would come back on a more suitable occasion, at low tide.

At last the eerie light began to fade, and he knew that outside, in the world of men and ships, darkness was closing in. He waited until it was quite dark. Then, lowering himself gently into the water, he groped for the passage. Having found it, he filled his lungs with air, and swimming under water struck out for the entrance. An area slightly less dark than the rest guided him, and within a minute he raised his head cautiously in the open starlit sea close to the foot of the cliff. He took a deep breath and listened. He could see nothing, but sounds of activity came from the cove where the submarine was moored. To these sounds he listened for a while, with a puzzled frown creasing his forehead.

It had been his intention, on emerging from his hiding place, as soon as he had ascertained that the coast was clear, to make a bee-line for the skiff, with the object of getting home with all possible speed. But as he listened to the noises in the adjacent cove, borne to his ears on the still night air, a horrible suspicion occurred to him. Such activity could only mean one thing. The submarine had completed its task of refuelling and was making ready for sea. If it succeeded in doing that all hope of destroying it would be postponed, if not entirely lost. The breeze had nearly died, as so often happens at nightfall; it would return at dawn, but that might be too late. As things were, he realized that it would take him a good four hours to reach the naval station and bring the U-boat destroyers to the spot. By that time the submarine would be well away among the numerous bays and reefs, and islets, that made U-boat hunting in the West Indies such a tiresome operation. No, he decided, that would not do. At any cost he must prevent that from happening.

A short swim took him to a shoulder of rock from which he was able to command a view of the cove. One glance and his suspicions were confirmed. The forward end of the submarine had already been cleared of camouflage. A man stood near the conning tower rapping out orders in a business-like way. There was no doubt that the U-boat would soon be leaving —at all events, would leave before dawn, otherwise the camouflage would have been left in place. What could be done about it?

Inspiration came to Jack like a brainwave, an idea so fantastic, so daring, that at first it took his breath away, and he was inclined to dismiss it. Still, he pondered, it might be done. It may have been that he could think of no other way of causing the U-boat's destruction that finally decided him to put the scheme into action. Another moment and he was swimming a powerful breast stroke to the nearest point where he could effect a landing. This was a beach where the cliff gave way to a sandy bay some hundred paces distant. Reaching a spot he made a brief but penetrating survey of the scene to make sure that the coast was clear, then dragged himself ashore. Another minute and he was among the palms that fringed the bay. Then he broke into a steady run towards the place where he had left the skiff.

It did not take him long to reach it, and to his infinite relief he saw that it was still there. All the way a horrid thought had persisted that the Nazis might have found it. Apparently they had concluded that he was dead.

He went straight to the engine locker, and from it took, first, a half-gallon can of lubricating oil, then a length of flex wire that he always carried for making repairs, splicing, and the like. With a screwdriver he made a small hole in the top of the can and another in the bottom. This done, he made one end of the wire fast to the handle of the can, and wound the rest of the wire round it. With the can under his arm he ran back to the beach where he had landed, and, slightly breathless from excitement at what lay before him, re-entered the water. Keeping close to the face of the cliff he swam gently towards the cove where the U-boat was moored.

In a few minutes he was in the cove, treading water, feeling his way along the edge of the rocks. Once he had a nasty moment when he saw a triangular dorsal fin cutting the water at no great distance, but he steeled himself, telling himself firmly that the shark might not be a man-eater.

He now began to swim under water, coming up to fill his lungs with air only when it became imperative, and then turning on his back so that only his face was exposed. In this way he neared the mass of palm fronds that formed most of the camouflage; much of it had now been thrown into the water, so that it provided him with useful cover. Under a large frond he paused to recover his breath and his composure. It was a weird sensation, for he was now within a few yards of the Nazis who were working on the U-boat's deck. Every word spoken came plainly to his ears, but of course the language used was German, which he did not understand, so he learned nothing from the conversations that went on. Gently, like an old crocodile in weeds round a water hole, he moved nearer, until at last his right hand touched the steel side of the underwater monster.

He now began to make his way towards the stern, using the same tactics that he had employed during his approach. That is to say, he allowed his body to sink, swam a little way—keeping touch with the U-boat—and then, turning on his back, floated up to refill his lungs. Towards the finish he had another shock when he collided with the propeller. For a nerve-shattering moment he thought it was the shark.

He had now reached his objective, the stern of the submarine, and he began to grope about over the steel hull for an object which he knew from pictures that he had seen of such craft was there; but he could not remember the exact position. At last he found it, one of the small steel rings that are used for making the submarine fast to mooring buoys, or piers. Or it may have been that the rings were used in case of emergency to lift the U-boat from the sea bed. It didn't really matter. The main thing was, the ring was there, and it did not take him long to tie the free end of the wire to it. Then he lowered the punctured oil can to the full length of the wire, and his immediate task was complete. All that remained now was to get to the naval base and tell the story. If the submarine should leave before he could bring the bombers to the spot—well, it did not matter, for wherever the U-boat went it would leave a tell-tale trail of oil. Unless his device was discovered, the submarine could no more free itself from the betraying stain than a fox can free itself of its taint.

He had just begun to move away when an order

was given, and a quantity of debris was thrown overboard. He did not know what it was, but something struck him on the head with sufficient force to make his senses reel. For a moment he clung to a palm frond, gasping; then, recovering, he began a careful withdrawal, using the same underwater tactics as before.

He was only just clear of the U-boat when a sudden commotion of the water literally flung him to the surface in a state not far from panic. Again, not unnaturally, his thoughts flashed to the shark. His first impression was that the monster had made a grab at him, and missed. But as the turbulance continued the truth dawned on him, and his nerves twitched at the narrowness of his escape. The submarine's powerful engines had been started, and the commotion in the water was caused by the propellers. Strangely, perhaps, the possibility of such a thing had not occurred to him; and now that the danger was passed he realized with a thrill of horror that had he been a few minutes later the churning steel blades would have cut him to pieces. As it was, he was helped by the water they now thrust behind them, and in a mass of broken palm fronds he was literally tossed against the beach. He did not mind; his satisfaction at the success of his plan rose above all other emotions. Dragging himself ashore he lay still for a moment to get his breath. By the time he had done this the U-boat was moving slowly towards the mouth of the cove. Everyone would be aboard, so as far as the island was concerned he had nothing to fear. Getting up, he set off at a run for the skiff.

Now that the immediate danger was passed, reaction set in, and he was conscious of a strange sensation of unreality. Time had become curiously telescoped. It seemed years since he had first spotted the U-boat. He had no idea of the hour, but he knew that it must be getting late. He also knew that his father would be getting alarmed at his non-return, for he was under a promise always to return at nightfall. However, this did not worry him unduly; when his father heard his amazing story he would understand.

The feel of the skiff as he launched it went far to reassure him. There was something so friendly, so normal, about it, that it brought him back to the world of reality, to the things of everyday life, things he knew and understood. He hauled up his sail, and started the motor, for the thing that mattered most now was speed. The submarine was already at sea, and a half gallon of oil would not last indefinitely. Dropping into his usual seat, and gripping the tiller, he headed for the open sea, and his island home.

Four hours later he ran the skiff against the landing stage of the Fleet Air Arm marine aircraft base. A sentry promptly challenged him, and he made haste to announce his identity. The sentry took him to the guardroom, where he found himself among some marines whom he knew. They fired questions at him, which was not surprising, for not until he stood under the bright electric light did he realize what a state he was in. His pants were torn. His body was bruised and smeared with oil. Blood oozed from a wound in his scalp, but he was in no mood to answer questions. He himself asked one. He was anxious to know the time, to know how long it would be until sunrise.

The sergeant of the guard looked at his watch and said that it was a quarter to five.

Jack was amazed. He had no idea that he had been so long away. It would start to get light in three quarters of an hour. "I want to see the station commander," he said.

The sergeant stared. "What! At this hour! You're crazy."

"Not so crazy as you'll be if you don't do as I ask," replied Jack.

"What's the big idea?" demanded the sergeant suspiciously.

"Only that I've got a German U-boat taped," answered Jack calmly.

"Blimy!" gasped the sergeant. "Fetch the orderly officer, Joe."

The orderly officer came. Jack repeated his request to be taken to the officer commander. The orderly officer was doubtful, but when Jack mentioned U-boat he made haste to oblige. He took Jack to the headquarters office, where, a few minutes later, the station commander, Captain Vane, R.N., appeared.

"What's all this about?" he demanded. "Why, it's young Cadet Carrington. What is it, Jack?"

Jack stood to attention. "I have to report, sir, that Porpoise Island is being used as a secret U-boat refuelling station. I've been there all day, watching one. The end of the pipe-line is under a cairn of rocks in the cove at the north east corner of the island."

The captain's manner changed. "You're sure of this?"

"Certain, sir. I actually touched the boat. The
156

There was no doubt that the U-boat would soon be leaving—at all events would leave before dawn.

What could be done about it?

crew saw me, and chased me. They fired at me, but I gave them the slip."

"Do you mean the U-boat is still there?"

"No, sir. It put to sea four hours ago."

The captain threw up his hands. "Confound it! Then we've lost it."

"I think not, sir," went on Jack. "Let me go in an aircraft and I think I can find it for you."

The captain looked incredulous. "Are you asking me to believe that you can work miracles?"

Jack smiled. "No, sir. But I mean what I say. This is my submarine and I want to see the end of it. It's better that it should be destroyed outside the cove."

"Why?"

"Because it is reasonable to suppose that other U-boats will come into the cove to refuel, and we ought to be able to catch them all in turn. If we made a mess inside the cove the others would take fright; they'd clear off and never come back."

"That's true," agreed Captain Vane. "But you're not really in the service, you know, and I have no authority to let a civilian go out on a war operation."

"That's just it, sir," protested Jack. "I want to prove to you, and the Commodore at Jamaica, that in spite of all you say about my age I'm not too young to be in the regular service. If you'll let me go I think I can promise you a kill."

"All right. You can go," decided the captain. "You can't go in a surface craft because they're all at sea. I shall send a flying-boat, with Lieutenant Hale as pilot, to locate the submarine. You can act as guide. If we can find the U-boat we'll soon have some ships on the spot."

"Thank you, sir," answered Jack fervently.

Then Captain Vane got busy.

Twenty minutes later the flying-boat left the water, with Lieutenant Tiny Hale at the control column. Jack sat beside him, with Captain Vane watching events from the navigator's table. Jack had still not divulged how he hoped to track the U-boat. Dawn was just breaking over a flat sea that shimmered with all the hues of mother-of-pearl. The wake cut by the aircraft as it took off flashed like a jewelled chain. A slight mist still hung over the land, shrouding it in a soft, lavender-tinted mantle. It was a charming picture, but Jack had no eyes for it. He was too engrossed with the work on hand. Now that the striking force was actually on the way he was fairly palpitating with excitement, although he did his best not to show it.

Captain Vane had, of course, communicated Jack's information to the higher authority, with whom he was still in touch by radio. Jack was not surprised, therefore, when presently he saw two destroyers, flinging up huge bow waves as they headed at full speed for Porpoise Island. A little later a corvette could be seen tearing the surface off the ocean as it tore along on the same course. Soon afterwards he saw two motor torpedo boats, streaking like greyhounds for the rendezvous. The navy had certainly wasted no time, thought Jack.

Under his direction Tiny made straight for the cove where the U-boat had been moored. The camouflage was still there—but no submarine. Not that Jack expected to see it. He pointed out the camouflage to the captain—no easy matter, for from the air it was hardly perceptible, and then stared at the open sea beyond the entrance to the cove. Instantly a shout of exultation, which he could not repress, rose to his lips.

"It worked!" he cried. "It worked!" With a quivering forefinger he pointed to a long smear that started at the cove and trailed away to the horizon. It was not straight, but wandered about apparently aimlessly, although this, Jack realized, was due to surface currents. "That's the way she went," he exclaimed.

This was so obviously true that no one denied it, and Tiny took up a new course along the track. The captain passed a message to the radio operator for transmission in code to the surface craft; then, with a puzzled expression on his face, he turned back to the trail.

"I never saw anything like that in my life," he declared. "The commander of that U-boat must be raving mad to put to sea in that condition, to leave a trail like that."

"I don't suppose he knows anything about it," murmured Jack.

"But he'd know if he had a buckled plate—and that's the only explanation I can think of to account for an oil track as conspicuous as that."

"That isn't caused by a buckled plate," chuckled Jack.

The captain looked at him curiously. "How do you know?"

"Because I happen to know what is causing it," asserted Jack, who was thoroughly enjoying himself.

The captain's eyes narrowed. "What did cause it?"

"My oil can," answered Jack.

"Your *what*!"

"Oil can," repeated Jack. "I tied a punctured can of oil to the U-boat's tail."

The captain stared as though he doubted the evidence of his ears and eyes, which is hardly to be wondered at. He looked at Tiny, who was laughing. "Can you beat that?" he breathed. Then, to Jack, he observed: "You must have had your nerve with you, my lad, when you played that trick. If those Germans had caught you they'd have skinned you alive."

"It wasn't the Jerries I was afraid of," said Jack seriously. "It was a perishing shark that came nosing round the cove while I was doing the job. He and I were in the water together, and it was a dashed uncomfortable feeling."

"I'll bet it was," asserted the captain warmly.

Nothing more was said, for all eyes were now on the trail.

"There she is!" cried Tiny sharply, as a black object appeared on the surface far ahead. "She's heard us—she's submerging," he added, as the speck disappeared.

"That won't help her if she's still got that oil can on her tail," said the captain grimly.

In five minutes Tiny had reached the spot where the U-boat had submerged. This was revealed by a sudden turn in the oil trail. The U-boat, having gone down, had evidently played the old trick of turning away sharply on a new course. But this did not help it. The oil still came floating up to mark the vessel's course as clearly as a chalk line on a blackboard. The U-boat could not be seen, but it was possible to mark its actual position by the stain. Obviously, the submarine was always just in front of where the oil came floating up. There was something awful, relentless, in the way the oil continued to rise.

Jack clutched at the side of the aircraft as Tiny put the machine in a dive that took it down to a thousand feet from the surface of the sea. Jack watched, fascinated, wondering what was going to happen next. He could hear the radio transmitter buzzing, sending out the signals that the captain passed to the operator—signals that had in them something of the awful inevitability of death. For the submarine was doomed—of that Jack had no doubt whatever. Looking through a side window he saw the destroyers, the corvette, and the motor torpedo boats racing for the spot where the aircraft was now circling.

"Hello, she's stopped," announced Tiny.

Looking down Jack saw that the stain had ended; but oil continued to rise, and spread out over the sea in an ever widening ring.

"She's sitting on the bottom, waiting for us to give up the hunt, little guessing that we know just where she is," said the captain. "Well, in war, you never know what's coming next. Go ahead, Tiny."

Tiny flew slowly over the centre of the circle of oil. A small object hurtled down. It struck the water with a splash, and at once erupted a plume of white smoke that drifted idly into the limpid air. Jack realized that he was marking the spot for the destroyers —a spot that was now certain to be the U-boat's grave. From his elevated position he had a grandstand view of the proceedings.

The destroyers raced up, and cut across the stain.

As they did so, barrel-shaped objects sprang from their decks, and after a curving flight landed in the sea. Jack had seen depth charges before, but this was the first time he had seen them used in action.

A great pillar of white water rose high into the air from the spot where the first depth charge had struck. It was only the beginning. Time and time again the water was lashed into foam and flung high into the air as the depth charges exploded beneath the surface. Then, out of the smother of foam, rose a large black object. It was the stern of the stricken U-boat with its propellers still turning slowly. For a moment it hung in the boiling water; then it slid forward and disappeared. The foam settled. In its place, a great turgid stain began to form, a stain that grew ever wider until it covered an area as large as a small island.

As in a dream Jack heard the captain say to Tiny: "I don't think there's much doubt about that one. The packet the boys gave her must have crumpled her like an eggshell. There won't be any survivors —there seldom are when you catch them on the bottom. Poor devils. There must have been a moment when they wondered how the deuce we found them —but they never knew."

Jack shivered. "I'm glad they didn't," he blurted.

The captain glanced at his pale face, and shrugged his shoulders. "Don't let it upset you," he said quietly. "Remember, that same crew has probably sent many a helpless merchantman to Davy Jones. Their turn was bound to come, sooner or later." He turned to the radio operator. "Send a signal to base to let them know it's all over. Give the boys a dip, Tiny."

Tiny flew over the now circling surface craft, and

dipped his wings in salute. "Now where to, sir?" he asked. "Back to the base?"

"Not just yet," replied the captain. "I'd like to have a look at this refuelling station, which, incidentally, should now be a first class trap. The boat we've sunk is not the only steel fish that uses the cove, I'll warrant. We should be able to catch them all, one by one, as they come in."

Jack smiled. "I won't promise to tie any more oil cans to their tails," said he.

Tiny laughed as he headed back for the island.

In a few minutes the big machine was floating lightly on the placid surface of the cove. Jack pointed out the nest of palm fronds under which the U-boat had hidden itself, and the cairn of rocks that concealed the end of the pipe line. He also told his story with more detail, pointing to the cliff from which he had made his desperate dive, and the cave in which he had hidden.

"I wonder the Jerries didn't spot that cave," said the captain, in some surprise.

"Ah, but it didn't look like that when I bolted in to it," answered Jack. "The tide was up then, and almost concealed it. Now the tide has ebbed it is far more conspicuous. I wasn't the first chap to use that cave," he went on, remembering the keg. "I fancy pirates used it—at any rate, there's an empty rum barrel there."

The captain looked thoughtful. "Is there, by Jove! That's interesting. Let's launch the dinghy and have a look at it."

Jack's second entry into the cave—or rather, caves, for there were several of them, all connected—was very different from his first visit. Sitting comfortably

163

in the dinghy, he and the captain, paddling with their hands, urged the little craft into the strange world beneath the cliff. Now that the tide was out there was much more elbow room, and more light, so that it was possible to see a number of ledges similar to the one on which Jack had rested.

Leaving the captain to examine the keg, which he declared his intention of keeping for a souvenir, Jack wandered on a little way and then pulled up with an exclamation of alarm.

"What is it?" asked the captain hurrying up.

Jack pointed to a skeleton that sat in a huddled position on the green coral.

"Poor wretch, he must have died here," remarked the captain. "I wonder why he stayed. If he got in, surely he could have got out."

"Look! He's lost a foot," muttered Jack. "I should say a shark took it. Perhaps that's why he stayed. The poor fellow must have sat here and bled to death, not daring to enter the water again."

As he finished speaking there was a sudden surge in the water that set green fire flashing. Just below the surface a long dark form, shaped like a torpedo, was moving slowly towards the entrance.

"Look! The shark!" cried Jack. "He's making for the entrance. This must be his lair." The colour drained from his face, and his legs went weak with shock, when he remembered that he had swum in that same water. He shuddered. "By gosh! Had I known that brute was in here, I reckon I should have stayed, too. No wonder the sailor couldn't get out."

The captain stooped and picked up a small object that lay near the skeleton. "Here's his knife," he

164

said. "It's an old fashioned one. This chap died a long time ago."

It was Jack's turn to stoop. He had noticed what appeared to be a small bundle, but when he went to lift it he was amazed at the weight. Then the fabric, which had evidently rotted where it had come in contact with the coral, burst, and a stream of gold coins spread out over the ledge.

For a moment Jack was too astonished to speak. The captain too, could only stare. In the end it was he who broke the silence.

"Well, I'll go hopping to Jericho!" he muttered. "Treasure trove, by jingo!"

"This must have been the origin of the legend about a pirate treasure," declared Jack, when he could find his tongue. "I've spent hours looking for it. Now, when I wasn't even thinking of it, I've found it."

The captain smiled. "With one thing and another it seems to have been your lucky day," he remarked. "But I mustn't play about here any longer. Pick up the doubloons and let's get away."

It was not a big treasure, as treasures go—just over a hundred gold coins of mixed nationalities, the result, no doubt, of many a bloody raid. But, as Tiny observed when they got back to the aircraft, it was better than a poke in the eye with a blunt stick.

On arrival at the base Jack presented everyone who had taken part in the attack on the U-boat with a gold piece, as a memento of the event.

What pleased Jack even more than the gold, was the letter he received shortly afterwards from the Admiralty, congratulating him on his praiseworthy behaviour—which, incidentally, resulted in the destruction of three more U-boats during the ensuing few weeks. Captain Vane also received a letter, one which, when he was informed of its contents, filled Jack's cup of happiness to the brim. It authorised the enlistment forthwith, into the Royal Navy, of Sea Cadet Jack Carrington, the only stipulation being that he was to remain on the strength of the unit at Trinidad for the time being.

With this Jack was well content, and thereafter, whenever his duties took him near Porpoise Island, as they often did, he waved it a greeting for giving him the chance of a lifetime.

A NIGHT OUT

Pilot Officer Kazi Mahomet, Royal Air Force, who learned the art of stalking in the jungle, finds his knowledge useful on a sabotage raid in Germany.

S Flying Officer Lance Lorimer, Royal Air Force, walked from his quarters towards the officers' mess, a hand was laid lightly on his arm.

"Hello," said a voice.

Lance stopped. Turning, he looked with faint surprise at a slim, youthful figure, in the same uniform as himself, with "wings" on the breast of his tunic and the rings of a pilot officer on his sleeves. But there the resemblance ended. Dark oriental eyes looked frankly into his own from a face that was the colour of a sun-dried river bed.

"Hello," said Lance. "What can I do for you?"

The other smiled. "You can let me go with you. I know your usual comrade was wounded on your last flight, so you will need a new partner."

Lance raised his eyebrows. "Go with me? Do you know the sort of work I do?"

"Of course," was the instant reply. "Everyone on the aerodrome knows that you land in enemy

167

country to do all sorts of jobs that couldn't be done any other way."

Lance considered the brown face with a puzzled smile. "What makes you think you are the man for such work?"

The other shrugged his shoulders. "I don't say that I am; but I would like to be. Unless I try I shall never know."

"That's true," agreed Lance. "You're from India, aren't you?"

The brown face broke into a smile, showing white teeth. "You should know."

Furrows of surprise lined Lance's forehead. "How should I know?"

"Don't you remember me?"

"I can't say that I do," confessed Lance.

"My father was subadar of B Company, in your father's regiment, in India. Afterwards 'he was of use'* as was your father. They died on the same day, fighting side by side for the honour of the regiment. We were boys when we last looked upon each other, at Delhi."

Recognition dawned in Lance's eyes. "Don't tell me you're Kazi . . . Kazi Mahomet?"

The other laughed softly. "The same. The places of our fathers are empty, but we are here to fill them."

Lance caught Kazi by the shoulders. "Kazi! This is wonderful. But how came you here?"

"I came to England seven years ago," answered Kazi. "I was at Oxford, studying to be a doctor. Then I heard about you, and what you were doing in the Royal Air Force. I thought I would like to do the same."

* In India, a regimental expression, meaning that he died fighting.

168

"Why didn't you write to me?"

"I was tempted to do so," admitted Kazi. "I thought if I did you would want to help me, but I preferred to make my own way through the flying school. Now I have qualified. I told the posting officer at the Air Ministry that I would like to be near you, and he, understanding—for he had served in India—was able to arrange the posting. All I ask now is that we may fly and fight together."

Lance looked doubtful. "Mine is dangerous work, Kazi."

Kazi drew himself up. "Since when did my people shrink from danger?"

"I didn't mean it like that, Kazi," returned Lance quickly. "I work alone—in the dark."

"Like the jungle folk?"

Lance smiled again. "The tricks your father taught me in jungle lore have more than once been my salvation."

"Was I not with you then? Give me a chance," pleaded Kazi. "Do you remember the day we took the polo ponies, and borrowing spears from your father's bungalow, ran down that old boar with the blood-red eye—the father of all hogs, was he. When your horse fell in the nullah, he would have cut you to pieces with his tushes had not my father followed us. Our places would have been empty that night, had it not been for him. Yet I did not turn from danger that day."

Lance's eyes danced at the memory. "Shall I ever forget it! I got a rare fright."

"Then our ambition was to kill a tiger," went on Kazi eagerly. "But now I would kill these beasts of men, these Nazis, who make war on women and

169

children, young and old, without mercy, and—hard though it is to believe—without giving warning. Let us hunt together again, with planes for horses and guns instead of spears. Think of the joy it will give our fathers to know that we ride in arms together, for the honour of the old regiment."

"You make it hard for me to say no, Kazi," said Lance uncomfortably. "You're rather young for such work. How old are you.?"

"Eighteen. But why speak of that? You are only a year older yourself."

"It's true I need a new partner, but the job on hand is not an easy one." Lance laughed. "Don't look so glum. Let's go in and have some coffee while I think about it."

In the mess, with coffee between them, they talked it over.

"Because I speak the language of the Germans, and because when I was young I learned to move at night without making a noise, I was selected for special work in enemy country," explained Lance. "Usually it is work of destruction—or, as we call it, sabotage. In a war like this there are times when one man, or two men, can do as much damage as an army. When it is dark I go. I strike. Then, like an old tiger who knows the meaning of gunshots, I return to cover."

"Are you going to Germany to-night?"

Lance filled the coffee cups before he answered. "Yes, I go to-night."

"And what is the task, if I may ask?"

Lance hesitated. "The only man who knows what I do is he who goes with me."

"Then let that man be me," put in Kazi quickly. "Give me one chance. If I do not acquit myself with credit I will never ask to come again."

"Very well. That's fair," agreed Lance. "But first I had better tell you about the sort of work I do; it may cause you to change your mind. If you still want to come after you have heard—well, you can't say I didn't give you fair warning. Generally speaking, I do jobs that can't be done any other way. They are not always the same. Sometimes I take secret agents into enemy occupied territory, men who know the country, to wreck the railways, block the roads, cut the telegraph wires, and do work of that sort. Sometimes I go to France, or Holland, or Norway, to bring home prisoners who have escaped. Sometimes I go to Poland, or Yugoslavia, to take ammunition to patriots who are still fighting the Nazis from hiding places in the mountains. Sometimes I meet these patriots in enemy country, and we do our best to make life miserable for the enemy." Lance smiled. "I'm rather like a leopard who stalks abroad in the night, looking for trouble."

"It sounds thrilling to me," asserted Kazi.

"Sometimes it's a bit too thrilling," declared Lance.

"What sort of plane do you use?" inquired Kazi.

"That's a secret," answered Lance mysteriously. "But if you are coming with me you will have to know about it. It's a special machine, of course; a small, fast, cabin two-seater, fitted with big flaps to make slow landings possible. Usually I have to find my own landing grounds, and they are not always good ones —at any rate, not for night work. Naturally, I study the map before I go, and sometimes our high-flying reconnaissance machines are able to provide me with photographs, which are a great help. I have such photographs for to-night's raid." Lance poured more coffee.

"And what is the job to-night?" asked Kazi, curiously.

"To-night," answered Lance, "I go to Linzberg, or to a place near that town, on the main railway line that runs from the Ruhr, in Germany, to Italy. The line is always in use, but our secret agents report that it is now being used more than ever to take men, guns, tanks, and ammunition of all sorts, to the enemy forces in North Africa."

"Why not bomb the line?" suggested Kazi.

"We have bombed it," answered Lance. "Unfortunately, a railway line can soon be repaired. But it happens that near Linzberg the line goes through a tunnel. If that tunnel could be destroyed —blown up with explosive, for instance—the line would be out of action for a long time."

"And that," said Kazi quickly, "is what you are going to do—blow up the tunnel?"

"That is what I hope to do," admitted Lance.

"By dropping a bomb on it?"

"No. That would be no use. The tunnel is too far under the ground. There is only one way of making absolutely certain of it, and that is to blow it up from the inside with a charge of high explosive. I take a special bomb with me."

"That means that you will have to go into the tunnel?"

"Of course."

Kazi smiled. "I begin to understand what you mean when you speak of dangerous work."

172

"I warned you."

"I did not say I objected to danger," protested Kazi.

"Then you still want to come?"

"More than ever."

"Very well. I'll see if I can fix it up."

"Tell me," asked Kazi. "How do you dress for this work? Do you go in disguise?"

"No. If I am to be shot, I prefer to wear my uniform. But over it I put on a long, dark raincoat, which serves to cover my uniform should occasion arise. In darkness, one raincoat is much like another. As I can speak German fluently, that is as much disguise as I need. More than once, at night, I have passed as a Nazi. You will have to wear such a coat if you come. Can you speak German?"

"A little," answered Kazi. "I understand the language better than I can speak it."

Lance looked surprised. "That's splendid."

"I was in Germany before the war, for a little while," explained Kazi. "I went to study chemistry, but I did not like the people—or perhaps they did not like me—so I came back. Tell me this. Do you make plans before you go?"

"Only up to a point. I have found that on these jobs it isn't much use making a plan because something usually arises to upset it. I find it better to make my plan when I get there, when I can see how the land lies."

"When do we start?"

"I shall leave the ground at seven o'clock to-night. The moon rises about ten. By starting at seven, we can fly over the worst of the enemy's defences in total darkness, yet have the moon to help us, should we need it, when we get to the objective."

"What about weapons?" asked Kazi.

"If all goes well we shan't want any," replied Lance. "I always take a Tommy-gun under the seat, though, and a few hand grenades—just in case. In my pocket I carry a revolver and a torch. You had better do the same." Lance glanced at the clock. "Time is getting on," he observed. "I'll go and tell the commanding officer that I've found a new partner. Then we'll have a look at the photographs, and the aircraft. By the way, it has a name that should appeal to you. I call it *Shikari*."

Kazi smiled. "Very appropriate," he agreed. "It will be like old times."

At seven o'clock that night the silence of the aerodrome was shattered as Lance started the engine and taxied out to take off. A minute later, after a signal from the duty officer, the *Shikari* was in the air, climbing into the starry sky on a course slightly south of east. Ahead, in the direction of the coast, long silver fingers probed the sky, but these were only the British defending searchlights. Once, one found and flashed on the wings of the *Shikari* as it continued to climb. The needle of the altimeter crept round the luminous dial—ten, twelve, fifteen thousand feet, and still the nose of the aircraft pointed upwards. Not until the needle rested on the twenty thousand mark did Lance put the machine on an even keel. At a signal from his navigation lights the questing beams vanished, leaving the sky darker than before.

Peering down, Kazi saw the dark shadow of the English coastline fading away astern. Another dark shadow appeared ahead—the vague, sinister shadow

174

of enemy territory, where a hundred million men, women and children, toiled under the Nazi task-masters. Far to the south, a group of swaying search-light beams, and crimson sparks of bursting shells, marked a spot where British bombers were pounding an enemy submarine base.

Lance moved his left hand, and the drone of the engine died away. The nose of the machine tilted down, and the *Shikari* glided on through the night with its slowly-turning airscrew muttering.

"I always glide through the coast defences," Lance told Kazi, who sat beside him. "There's less chance of our being heard, or seen. Our intruder patrols will be busy lower down, shooting up the German aerodromes, so I hope the enemy will be too busy with them to notice us."

As they glided on, Kazi watched the ground—or what little he could see of it. Of the perilous nature of the task for which he had volunteered, he had no delusions. Apart from the risk of being shot down by enemy guns, or hostile fighters, there was the difficult business of landing in unknown country; a miscalculation would mean that at best they would be prisoners in the hands of the enemy for the duration of the war. A bad landing might explode the heavy charge of high explosive contained in a square box under the seat. Yet the landing was only the beginning. After that would come the most dangerous work of all—the journey on foot across enemy soil, and the demolition of the tunnel.

Below, the earth was wrapped in profound darkness. No details could be seen, except occasionally a forest, lying like a black stain across the landscape, or a pale, winding ribbon, that marked the course of a road or river. Occasionally, the flickering white finger of a searchlight quartered the sky, but Lance had little difficulty in avoiding it. Once, when one stabbed the darkness uncomfortably close to a wing-tip he slipped sideways in a steep turn.

After about ten minutes Lance said: "I think we're through the worst, but keep a sharp watch for prowling Messerschmitts." He opened the throttle; the nose came up, and the *Shikari* raced on through the night.

After that, Kazi lost count of time. The flight, like all long-distance flights, seemed interminable. He felt that he had been in the air for hours. Beside him Lance sat with expressionless face, his eyes some-times probing the loneliness around them, sometimes studying the instruments.

At last, after peering down, he gave a grunt of satisfaction and pointed. "Look!" he said, "there's the railway."

For some moments Kazi had difficulty in finding it. The landscape, shrouded in darkness, all looked alike. Overhead, here and there a star showed mistily through a thin layer of cloud, and a pale glow over the horizon, beyond the swirling arc of the airscrew, showed the position of the rising moon; but deep night still lay across the land. Only by staring hard could he just make out a faint black line, as straight as an arrow, running across the sombre background of the earth. As they sank lower, more details could be seen—roads, woods, and rivers. Once a light showed for a moment, flashing like a diamond on black velvet, but there was no indication of what had caused it.

Kazi experienced a twinge of uneasiness as the mutter of the engine died away. The airscrew stopped.

The only sound now was the faint sigh of air over the plane. They were going down, which meant that Lance had picked out his landing ground. Glancing at him, he saw that a photograph lay on his knees, in the glow of the luminous dials on the instrument board.

"Do you know where we are?" asked Kazi, realizing with a pang of disappointment that he still had much to learn before he could undertake such a mission alone.

"Yes. I think we're all right," answered Lance, and again turned his attention to the ground.

The *Shikari* tilted over on its wing, and the inky void beneath seemed to rise to meet them. Then, suddenly, the machine was on even keel, skimming the tree-tops. Kazi held his breath, knowing that everything now depended on the pilot's skill in making a landing. Lower—lower—lower, dropped the machine. The wheels touched, bounced a little, and then ran on. The tail-skid dragged. The wheel-brakes made the machine vibrate a little as they brought it to a stop. Instantly Lance opened a side window, and then sat listening intently. All was silent except for the usual distant noises of civilization —the whistle of a train, and the rumble of a motor vehicle. Yet somehow these sounds were sinister to Kazi, possibly because he knew they were being made by the enemy. He felt a prickling sensation under his skin, a feeling he had not known since the first time he had sat up under the jungle moon to watch a tiger return to its kill. With parted lips and straining eyes he stared into the gloom around the machine.

"Everything seems nice and quiet," said Lance softly. "Let's get out. Don't make a noise."

They stepped out on to the turf, and stood listening intently. Not a sound broke the silence.

"Fine," whispered Lance. "Let's get the old *Shikari* under the trees on the edge of the field, where it will be less likely to be seen. I always leave it with the nose pointing to the open field, in case I have to get off in a hurry."

Slowly and deliberately they dragged the machine by the tail across the dew-soaked turf into the deep shadow of a group of pines that fringed the field. Lance lifted the explosive from the cockpit and put it gently on the ground.

"You looked at the photo before we started, so you should know where we are," he told Kazi. "This is the field we decided on. The railway cutting runs through the forest you can see on the far side. I reckon the northern mouth of the tunnel is about four hundred paces from the edge of the trees."

"Will there be sentries?" breathed Kazi.

"I don't know," replied Lance. "We shall have to behave, though, as if there was a guard at the tunnel." He picked up the box of explosive. "Come on."

For ten minutes they made steady progress, sometimes stopping to listen to sounds that came faintly through the still night air. Once, the shrill cry of a nighthawk made Kazi's heart miss a beat. Shortly afterwards Lance laid a hand on his arm.

"If we haven't lost our bearings there should be a crossroads just ahead. That will give us our exact position."

They crept on, and crawling through a gap in the hedge saw the crossroads before them. The moon was now clear of the trees, and visibility was improving.

"S-s-h," breathed Lance. "I can hear something

coming. It sounds like a car. We had better let it go past."

They crouched back in the hedge as twin sparks of light, the screened headlights of a car, came slowly down the road. Reaching the crossroads, to Kazi's consternation, the vehicle stopped. There was silence for a moment. Then a door swung open and a man stepped out on to the road. Kazi could see a coal-scuttle helmet silhouetted against the light of the rising moon. The man spoke, in German, to an unseen companion.

"According to the operator of the new plane detector, this should be the place," he said. "Anyway, according to his calculations, the plane landed somewhere in this district. All the same, it's hard to know where to start looking. It would take a regiment to search all these fields and woods."

"The plane may not have landed," answered another voice. "The English are dropping spies everywhere, we know, but usually they come down by parachute."

"The operator did not hear the machine go back; that's why he thinks it must have landed," said the first speaker.

"So!" was the reply. "I don't see that two of us can do much in the dark."

"I agree with you there, Fritz," went on the other. "We'll go on quietly down the road towards Linzberg, and check up on any strangers we overtake."

The man got back into the car, which went on slowly down the road.

Kazi relaxed. "Phew!" he gasped. "That was a bit of a strain. I could nearly have touched that German."

"You'll get used to it," answered Lance, calmly. "You heard what they said? The Germans have evidently got a new sound detector, and it picked us up. They suspect we are about, so we shall have to be extra careful."

"Suppose they find the plane while we are away?" queried Kazi anxiously.

"If they do, I'm afraid it will be just too bad," answered Lance evenly. "Let's push on and get the job done." He took out a pocket compass and set a course. "I'm going to make straight for the northern end of the tunnel," he announced. "Keep your eyes and ears open for sentries."

After a careful survey of the road, with infinite caution they crept forward into the inky shadow of the forest. Kazi now had to carry the explosive charge in order to leave Lance's hands free to check their course by the compass. They stopped often to listen. The strain imposed by this sort of progress was worse even than Kazi expected. At any moment he expected to hear the sharp challenge of a sentry, and see the flash of his rifle as he fired.

"We're getting close," whispered Lance in Kazi's ear. "Notice how the trees are thinning in front of us. That clear space must mark the edge of the railway cutting. Don't make a sound." Lance put the compass in his pocket, and dropping to his knees began crawling. Kazi did the same, lifting his dangerous parcel in front of him.

"*S-s-h!*" Lance sank flat on the ground, and lay as still as death.

Kazi followed. A twig had snapped. It was only a slight noise, but he knew that twigs rarely snap by themselves. Then, as he lay listening, he heard

180

footsteps approaching. A figure loomed darkly against the moonlight ahead, where the trees ended. It stopped. In the profound silence Kazi was afraid that the man would hear the thumping of his heart. His lips went dry with shock when he realized that had it not been for the snapping of the twig they might have walked into the sentry. The sentry was a fool. Had he been trained in jungle lore he would not have broken the twig. Kazi's lips curled in faint derision, but his nerves jumped when the man spoke. His tone was normal, but in the silence it sounded like a thunder-clap. "Is that you, Rudy?" he asked.

"*Ja*, Willy," answered another voice, so close that Kazi flinched.

"Come on. You're five minutes late, as usual," growled the man named Willy.

"No, I am on time," argued the other. "I must admit, though, that I am not looking forward to four hours in this miserable place. I've been here for months, and I haven't seen a spy yet. Who cares about the tunnel?"

There was a crashing of bushes, and another figure loomed up. The two sentries met.

"There's another ammunition train coming along presently," said the one who had just arrived.

"I'm tired of looking at ammunition trains," muttered the other.

"The first speaker sighed. "Well, I'll get along to the guard-house and see if there is anything left to eat. Good night. Let me know if you find a spy."

The other laughed harshly. "You bet I will. *Gootnacht.*"

One of the figures disappeared; his footsteps could be heard receding along the railway line. The new sentry yawned, unfastened the collar of his tunic, hung his steel helmet on a twig and leaned his rifle against the tree. It was clear that he apprehended no danger.

Kazi lay still while minutes passed. The man showed no signs of moving. It looked as if he intended remaining there. Leaning against the tree he began to hum a tune.

Kazi cupped his hands round his mouth and put them against Lance's ear. "He intends to stay," he breathed.

"Yes," agreed Lance, speaking in the same way.

"We can't stay here all night. I think I can get him," went on Kazi. "Shall I try?"

"Yes."

Kazi braced himself. In all his experience of jungle craft he had never known a thrill quite like this. The work must be done silently, he knew. One sound and they were lost. One shot would be enough to start a general alarm.

Inch by inch, with the muzzle of his revolver gripped in his right hand, he wormed his way towards the unsuspecting sentry, who yawned again, as if he found his vigil wearisome. How long it took Kazi to get into position behind him he never knew. It seemed like hours, but it was the only safe way. At last he was so close that by reaching out he could have touched the man. Instead, his left hand groped in the loose earth until it found a small pebble. He tossed it a few yards beyond the sentry. It fell with a slight rattle on the dry pine needles.

The sentry started, peering in the direction of the sound. "Who's that?" he called crisply.

Kazi rose up behind him like a shadow and brought

182

the butt of his revolver down on the unprotected head.

The sentry croaked. He sagged at the knees, and crumpled on the ground without another sound.

Lance, carrying the parcel, joined Kazi. "Good work," he whispered. "Come on."

Quiet though they had been, they had evidently made a slight noise, for as they reached the edge of the cutting a voice spoke from the other side. With a pang of disappointment Kazi realized that this must be another sentry.

"What's the time, Rudy?" called the voice.

With a shock Kazi realized that the man was speaking to the sentry who now lay unconscious. If there was no answer he would wonder why.

"The time is a quarter past eleven," said Lance loudly, in German, imitating the fallen man's voice fairly well.

Somewhere in the distance, to the north, an engine whistled, and a moment later there came the rumble of an approaching train.

"Here comes the ammunition," called the voice opposite.

"*Ja*," growled Lance. Then he turned swiftly to Kazi. "This is our chance," he whispered tersely. "The noise of the train will drown any noise we make. We'll wait for it to get closer, then make a dash for the tunnel. If we can get the train at the same time there should be a pretty display of fireworks."

"What about the other sentry?" asked Kazi anxiously.

"You'll have to take care of him—but only if he sees us and tries to interfere."

"All right."

The train was now about a quarter of a mile away,

183

making a good deal of noise—or so it seemed after the silence. Kazi could see the crimson glow of the furnace as the firemen stoked up. There was no time for more. Lance, crouching low, began running along the edge of the cutting, which became deeper, and after a short distance ended above a black hole which Kazi knew must be the mouth of the tunnel.

Lance snatched a glance at the approaching train. "We've no time to lose," he rapped out.

Slipping and sliding he scrambled down the steep slope, with the explosive in his left hand, and made for the tunnel. Kazi was at his heels. Like rabbits racing for a burrow they made for the yawning hole in the earth.

When they were within ten yards a blaze of light fell across the track, and pulling up in consternation Kazi saw that the door of a hut had been thrown open. He realized instantly what had happened, for a German, rifle in hand, stood in the doorway. This was the guard hut, used by the sentries when they were off duty. A shout told him that they had been seen.

Lance's voice rose above the noise of the approaching train. "Hold them, Kazi!" he shouted, and raced on towards the tunnel.

Suddenly perceiving his danger, for he was standing in the open, Kazi jumped to the side of the hut. A rifle blazed, and he felt the wind of the bullet on his cheek. His revolver cracked, and the man who had fired lurched forward, to fall in a heap across the track. Another man took his place. Running in closer, Kazi fired again. The man dropped his rifle, and sank to his knees beside his fallen companion.

184

Other figures could be seen moving against the lamp-light inside.

Although he was outnumbered, Kazi realized that he held one big advantage, and he took care to keep it. The Germans were in the light, and he was in the dark. Therefore, as each German tried to leave, he saw him before he himself could be seen. The men inside seemed to realize this, too, and they hung back. Above the noise of their shouting rose the roar of the train as it entered the cutting.

Kazi increased the panic inside the hut by firing three shots into the lighted doorway, and his lips parted in a mirthless smile as he realized that the enemy had no idea of how many men were outside. Out of the corner of his eye he saw Lance dash out of the tunnel, unwinding a coil of wire from a spool as he ran. The train whistled. A rifle flashed somewhere on the top of the cutting. The men in the hut shouted. To Kazi, the whole business began to assume the fantastic proportions of a nightmare. He saw Lance scrambling up the bank, beckoning furiously, so he backed away, intending to join him. But in the turmoil he forgot something—the railway lines. His heel struck one, and he fell across the track in front of the train. As he scrambled wildly to his feet he saw men rush out of the hut, saw two of them stumble and fall. Turning to the embankment he caught a fleeting glimpse of Lance, sitting on the bank, emptying his revolver at the hut. Panting with excitement and exertion he tore up the bank, just as the train roared past, between them and the hut.

Lance said only one word. It was "Run!"

Kazi needed no second invitation. He ran for his life; but as the train disappeared into the tunnel

Lance stopped.   Keep your head down!" he yelled, and then did something with a small instrument that he held in his left hand.

The next instant came—or so it seemed to Kazi—the end of the world. At first there was a single sharp detonation, but it was followed immediately by an explosion that rocked the earth; with it came a blast of air that sent trees crashing, and made breathing impossible. For a full minute the roar persisted, like a continuous roll of thunder, while the heavens were lighted up by a brilliant orange glare that made the landscape as light as day. Then the light faded, and the terrifying roar was succeeded, first by a clatter of rolling debris, then by an ominous silence.

Slightly dazed, and conscious of a strange feeling of unreality, Kazi raised his head, and looked upon such a scene of destruction that he could not have imagined. The mouth of the tunnel had completely disappeared. So had the guard hut. The entire edge of the forest had been lain flat. Above the tunnel the earth lay like a wilderness stricken by an earthquake; over it a cloud of smoke rose like a gigantic feather.

Lance touched Kazi on the arm. "A nice job," he said briefly. "This is going to stir things up a bit. In a minute or two this place will be buzzing like a hornets' nest. We'd better see about getting home."

"Yes, I think we've done enough for one night," agreed Kazi.

Lance laughed grimly. "It isn't over yet," he muttered, and set off at a run along the top of the cutting to get round the area of fallen trees and by way of the crossroads to the field where they had left the *Shikari*.

Long before they reached the road it became abundantly clear that Lance's prediction about the place buzzing like a hornets' nest was understatement rather than exaggeration. From all sides came the roar of motor vehicles, cars and cycles. Lights could be seen heading for the spot.

"I only hope they haven't got dogs," muttered Lance, as they ran on.

"Dogs—what dogs?" panted Kazi.

"The Nazis usually have dog patrols—or rather, hounds; ferocious brutes, trained for man-hunting. I've had one or two goes with them, and it's not a nice experience."

"Oh," said Kazi. "Think of something else unpleasant. How will the hounds pick up our scent?"

"They're trained to follow the taint of any strangers, and they might pick up ours on the road," explained Lance. "Unfortunately we can't get back to the aircraft without crossing the road."

Hardly had the words left his lips when over the night air came two sharp excited bays.

"That's it," murmured Lance. "They've picked up our tracks near the crossroads. If they follow them to the railway it will be all right, but if they back-trail us to the machine, things are going to be difficult. Keep going—it's no use stopping."

They reached the road, and ducked for cover as a high-powered car tore past. The moment it had gone they went on, only to shrink back against the hedge as a searchlight stabbed the sky, casting a pale, eerie glow, over the landscape. In a minute four beams were "coned" over the area, making it dangerously light and forcing them to remain close against the hedge. Shouts, and the blast of whistles, came from all sides. Twigs and branches crashed as they were trampled underfoot.

"They didn't lose much time getting here," muttered Lance. "They know, of course, that the tunnel didn't blow itself up, and they are also aware that the people who did the job must still be in the district. Time is everything now. Every minute will bring more troops to the spot. Whether we are seen or not we shall have to run for it, and we may have to fight it out. Have your gun ready."

Revolver in hand Lance set off at a run along the hedge that bounded the landing field, making for the belt of trees under which the aircraft had been parked. And for a time they did so well that Kazi hoped they would reach the machine without being molested. But this was not to be. He heard the hound coming along behind them before he saw it. Whether it had broken loose, or had been released to hunt on its own account, he did not know, but he knew the animal was there. With a soft patter of pads it ran into sight, looking enormous in the half-light. It threw up its head and bayed when it saw its quarry.

Kazi shouted a warning to Lance of the danger, and turning, levelled his reolver. But either the animal sensed danger, or knew what a revolver was, for it stopped, growling deep in its throat. This, apparently, was heard by the Nazis, for there were shouts of encouragement, followed by the thump of running feet.

"It looks as if we shall have to shoot our way out," said Lance calmly, as they ran on. "If I fall, don't stop for me. Keep on. Your only chance will be the machine. It is vital that our people at home should know that the tunnel has gone."

They were now within a hundred paces of the

Kazi needed no second invitation.
He ran for his life;
"Keep your head down" yelled Lance
and did something with a small
instrument he held in his left hand.

Shikari; indeed, Kazi could just see the faint outline of the aircraft in the reflected light of the searchlights. A rifle cracked, and a bullet tore a furrow in the turf. Another shot cut a twig from an overhanging bush. Glancing over his shoulder Kazi saw that two men were almost at their heels, and behind them, a line of running men, strung out like horses at the end of a long race. His cry of consternation made Lance look round.

"We can't do it," decided Lance. "We shall be in full sight and under fire, before we get clear. There's one chance. I'll hold them while you get to the machine and get the engine going. If I can do that you may be able to give me covering fire until I join you."

"But I can't leave you here," protested Kazi.

"You've got your orders," snapped Lance, and whirling round he faced the pursuers. A hound was almost on them. His revolver spat. The animal fell, but was on its feet in an instant, snarling furiously. Lance fired three quick shots at the men behind. One fell, and the others took cover in the hedge, from where they opened a rather erratic fire, enough, however, to force Lance to take cover in the hedge.

By this time Kazi had reached the *Shikari*. In desperate haste he hauled out the Tommy gun. By the time he had got it, and turned, Lance was retiring backwards along the hedge, using his revolver. At that moment, with a yell, the Nazis broke cover and charged.

The harsh staccato chatter of the Tommy gun cut in above the other sounds. It was like a live thing in Kazi's hands, and filled him with a feeling of fierce exultance. "Come on, Lance!" he yelled.

The next two minutes were pandemonium. Lance

189

made a dash for the machine. Shots whistled in both directions, some hitting the aircraft, but apparently the Nazis did not feel inclined to face the murderous fire that Kazi poured at them.

"Hold them for another thirty seconds!" shouted Lance, as he took a flying leap into the cockpit. "Get aboard as soon as the motor starts," he flung back over his shoulder.

From the cabin door Kazi continued to rake the hedge in short but deadly bursts. He heard the self-starter *whirr*; with a roar the engine came to life. He waited for no more, but threw himself into the cabin just as the machine began to move. From the floor he fired again until his gun was empty. It was a mad moment. Rifles flashed all along the hedge. Bullets ripped and tore through wood and canvas, but none, apparently, caused vital damage, for the *Shikari* raced on at ever increasing speed. The vibration of the wheels died away, and Kazi knew they were in the air. He closed the door, and leaving the empty gun on the floor, dropped with a gasp of relief into his seat beside Lance.

"Phew!" he panted, wiping perspiration from his forehead. "We've done it! You were certainly right when you talked about hot work."

Lance grinned. "The searchlights will find us presently, and then the fun will *really* begin. No doubt the radio is warning Messerschmitts all along our course home to be on the lookout for us."

"Think of something else," groaned Kazi.

"No, I think that's about all," replied Lance evenly. "You invited yourself to the party, don't forget."

"I'm not complaining," protested Kazi.

"You're doing fine," complimented Lance, as he zig-zagged like a snipe low over the trees to dodge the searchlights.

"If we are attacked by fighters we have nothing to fight back with," pointed out Kazi.

"This is not intended to be a fighting aeroplane," Lance reminded him. "We leave the fighting to the Spitfires, the Hurricanes and the Typhoons. Our job is to strike, like an old leopard, in the dark, and then get away without being caught. That's why—like a leopard—the *Shikari* is built for manœuvrability and speed. Unless we are cut off, we ought to be able to show any intercepting night fighters a clean pair of heels. Now we are clear of these searchlights I'm going to climb. Keep your eyes open and tell me if you see anything."

Kazi knew that the sound-detectors would be listening, so he was not surprised when, a few minutes later, "flak" tore the sky with flame and hurtling metal. But the shooting was poor, and he suspected that the enemy were putting up a blind barrage, trusting more to luck than judgment for a hit. Only once did he hear the vicious *whoof* of an explosion above the noise of the motor, and that one, he knew, was close enough to be really dangerous.

Searchlights sprang up from time to time. They had a disconcerting knack of leaping up out of the darkness, like a path of fire. But Lance knew all the tricks, and when this happened he employed them, cutting his motor, turning away, and side-slipping end-on to present the smallest amount of surface to the beams.

It was not until they were nearing the coast that Kazi saw his first enemy fighter, a Messerschmitt 109.

They were skimming along over a layer of high cloud at the time. Suddenly the cloud became luminous as searchlights struck it on the underside. From out of the luminous vapour appeared a dark form, followed by two more, looking rather like sharks swimming in a moonlit sea. Kazi warned Lance, and was still watching the Nazi fighters, which so far had not seen the *Shikari*, when, through a break in the clouds, a searchlight beam struck him full in the face, temporarily blinding him with its radiance. It was a nasty moment. He felt the machine swerve wildly as Lance dragged it clear of the beam, and waited for the grunting of multiple machine guns that would tell him they had been detected. But the sound did not come, and when Kazi was able to see again he understood what had happened. Grey vapour swirling past the side windows told him that Lance had taken cover in the cloud.

What became of the three enemy fighters he did not see, but soon afterwards the cloud ended abruptly, and as they shot out into clear air Lance had to bank vertically to avoid collision with another machine that was making for the cloud from the opposite direction. Kazi caught a fleeting glimpse of a black shape, and exhausts streaming flame, and then the machine had gone. But it did not go far. Looking back, he saw the Nazi turn, and come tearing along behind them. Again he warned Lance of the danger; not that the warning was necessary, for red tracer bullets flashing past the *Shikari's* wings told their own story.

Kazi felt the fighting spirit heat his blood. "Let's go for him!" he shouted.

Lance smiled, as he pressed on the control column,

and the *Shikari* sped on like a startled foal. "He has eight guns and we have none," he said. "On such jobs as this our duty is to get home and report what we have done, leaving the fighting to those who are armed for it. An old boar is brave, none braver, but even he, being wise, runs for cover when he is out-matched. We can show this fellow our heels." As he finished speaking Lance turned sharply into another cloud, and Kazi saw the Messerschmitt no more.

Minutes passed, during which he could only stare at the vapour that enveloped the little aircraft like a blanket. Lance kept the control column forward, so that the *Shikari* continued to lose height. More than once the mist turned red, or orange, as shells, fired by the ground batteries, burst near the machine.

"We're running through the defences over the French coast!" shouted Lance.

A few minutes later Kazi uttered a cry of satisfaction as the aircraft broke through the cloud into clear air; for there, a few hundred feet below, lay the sea, as placid as a mountain pool, glistening faintly where the starlight touched it. He smiled. "Our troubles are over," he exclaimed.

"A night pilot's troubles are never over until he is on the ground," corrected Lance. "I'm afraid I can *smell* trouble."

Kazi sniffed. "Petrol!" he cried as the reek of spirit struck his nostrils.

"Either a bullet from that Messerschmitt, or a shell splinter, got us through the tank," announced Lance calmly.

Kazi looked worried. "What can we do about it?"

Lance shrugged his shoulders. "Nothing." He kept the machine on its course.

193

"How far are we from home?" asked Kazi.

"Thirty miles."

"Then we ought to be home in a few minutes?"

"If the petrol lasts."

Kazi smiled at this casual announcement. Being a pilot, he knew that the flight was likely to end in one of three disasters. The worst was, the *Shikari* might catch fire at any moment, due to the escaping petrol being ignited by the exhaust. If this did not happen, and the petrol ran out, they would either finish up in the sea, or crash somewhere on the darkened countryside. Yet his sensation at that moment was not fear but disappointment, that having come so far, and having escaped so many dangers, they were likely to end ingloriously so near to home.

Glancing at the height indicator he saw that they were only five hundred feet above the sea. Then he stared fixedly ahead, at the point where the English coast should appear, counting the minutes as they passed, knowing that each one took them nearer to safety. And as he watched he saw the dark outline of the coast take shape. He was just beginning to hope that they might get through after all, when the engine coughed, spluttered, and after a violent backfire, stopped.

"That's it," said Lance, cheerfully, as he put the *Shikari* into a glide, "kick your shoes off, Kazi. I'm afraid we're going to get our shirts wet."

For a little while the *Shikari* glided on towards the coast, some details of which could now be seen; then it struck the cold face of the water in a cloud of spray. At the last moment Lance had snatched the control column back into his stomach, so the aircraft did not dive straight in, or turn over. It struck the

194

water with its belly, and remained afloat, held up by the air in the wings and the empty tank. They both scrambled out of the cabin and perched on a wing.

"Bad luck," said Kazi ruefully.

"We're not finished yet," announced Lance. "These coastal waters are alive with our patrol boats. Let's see if we can bring one along." As he spoke he groped in his pocket and took out a signalling pistol. Pointing it at the sky he sent a red flare soaring upward. He allowed a minute to pass, during which the *Shikari* settled a little deeper in the water, and then fired another.

"How long shall we float?" asked Kazi.

"A few minutes—long enough for someone to come along," answered Lance confidently.

As it happened, he was right, but the motor boat arrived only just in time. They were squatting on the wing, with the rest of the aircraft awash, when the powerful purr of the boat reached their ears.

Kazi pointed to a dark spot that was cutting a creamy scar across the surface of the sea. "Here she comes!" he cried.

A minute later the speed boat swept alongside, and a voice called cheerfully: "All right, boys. The Navy's here. Is there any chance of saving the machine? We're not far from the beach."

"Throw us a line and we'll try it," answered Lance. "If she goes down you can pick us up."

A rope coiled through the air like a black snake. Lance caught it deftly and made it fast. "Go ahead," he ordered. "Take it quietly."

The patrol boat made its way steadily towards the shore, and a few minutes later the aircraft was in the shallow water that fringed a gently shelving beach.

Bluejackets jumped into the water and hauled the machine high and dry.

"She'll be all right there," Lance told Kazi. "If we can find a telephone we'll soon have a working party here to take the old *Shikari* home."

They thanked their rescuers, who gave them a drink of hot coffee from a vacuum flask, and then made their way to the road that ran along the top of the beach. Here they were challenged by troops who, when their identity was established, took them to the nearest military headquarters, where a telephone enabled them to get in touch with their base aerodrome.

"The C.O. is sending a car for us," said Lance, as he hung up the instrument.

That is really the end of the story. An hour later they were back on the aerodrome where, in the officers' mess, they found coffee and food waiting for them. As they helped themselves, Lance turned to Kazi with a smile.

"Well, what do you think of my job now?" he inquired.

"Tiger shooting is tame sport compared with Nazi hunting," declared Kazi.

"Then you'd like to carry on with me?" asked Lance.

"That's what I'm hoping," admitted Kazi.

"In that case," replied Lance, "you can reckon it is fixed. You are the very partner I was looking for. Between us we ought to cause the Nazis quite a lot of trouble. As soon as the old *Shikari* has been overhauled we'll have another night out. What are you smiling at?"

"I was only thinking," answered Kazi slowly, "how our fathers must have chuckled over this night's work."

STORY
6

A "ROUTINE JOB"

A Story Of The Commandos

FROM twelve thousand feet Lieutenant Nigel Steer, of the Fleet Air Arm, looked down upon the placid surface of the Mediterranean Sea, only breaking his scrutiny to glance from time to time at a faint smudge, far to the north, that marked the position of the Italian island of Sicily. For a time he flew on, without observing anything remotely resembling the enemy submarine for which he was searching, but in the end his vigilance was rewarded.

He stiffened slightly in his seat as a minute speck on the blue water caught his eye, and he moved his head to make sure that it was not a spot of oil on the windscreen, as sometimes happened. The speck was still there. In a moment he had turned the nose of his Osprey seaplane towards it, at the same time cutting the engine and putting the machine in a shallow glide.

In three minutes the speck had taken shape, and he grunted his disappointment. Far from being the enemy submarine which was known to be in the vicinity, it turned out to be a tiny surface craft—

a canoe, he thought. He decided to go lower, to see who this could be, alone in a lonely sea, but before doing so caution prompted him to study the sky carefully, section by section, for hostile aircraft, before making himself vulnerable. And it was well that he did so. Far away to the north he made out another speck, turning in wide circles, so high that it looked like a mosquito crawling on a blue ceiling.

Nigel forgot the canoe. Settling himself a little lower in his seat, and taking a firmer grip of the control column, he roared up into the eye of the sun. That is to say, he put his aircraft in line between the circling machine and the sun, a position in which it was unlikely to be seen by the newcomer, who would have the sun in his eyes. Not for a moment did he take his eyes off the other aircraft, which presently resolved itself into an Italian Caproni fighter.

By the time he had gained his desired position in the sun the Caproni was losing height, and very soon it was going down in a steep dive towards the sea. Nigel remembered the canoe, and understood. It was clear that the enemy pilot had also seen the canoe; and from the manner of his approach Nigel suspected that the Italian had actually been looking for the little craft. The affair was becoming interesting, and for the moment he was content to watch.

But he did not watch for long; for what he saw was the last thing he expected. The occupant of the canoe was obviously in no condition to defend himself against an onslaught from the air, and even though the Caproni was going down it did not at first occur to Nigel that the Italian might use his guns. His surprise, therefore, when he saw tracer bullets churning the water into foam round the canoe, was only ex-

198

ceeded by his anger. This was not war. It was sheer murder. In an instant he was thundering down in the wake of the Caproni.

At this juncture the Italian pilot evidently saw him, for he suddenly broke off his attack on an opponent who could not fight back, in a desperate attempt to escape from one who could. The effort was short-lived. With the advantage of initial speed, the result of his terrific dive, Nigel swiftly overtook the Italian and forced him to turn. But the Italian apparently had no stomach for the fight, and thought only of escape—which in air combat is usually fatal. Thus it was in this case. For perhaps a minute the two machines raced round in an ever closing circle; then a lightning turn brought Nigel's sights to bear; short, jabbing tongues of flame, spurted from his guns; bullets flashed across the blue to end at the Caproni's nose. The engine vomited a cloud of oily black smoke. From its heart an ever-growing flame licked hungrily.

Nigel ceased firing, expecting to see the Italian use his parachute. But this, it seemed, he was unable to do. Possibly he had been hit by a bullet. At any rate, the aircraft went into a vertical dive from which it never recovered. A feather of foam leapt high into the air as it struck the sea. When the foam settled the Caproni was no longer there. Only a spreading stain of oil, and a few pieces of fabric, marked the spot where it had been.

Nigel turned away, looking for the canoe, which he soon saw about a mile distant. Gliding lower, he circled over it. The only navigator stood up and waved his paddle, but then sank down as if the effort had been too much for him.

Nigel put the Osprey lightly on the water beside the frail craft and raised himself in his seat. From this position he was able to see that the paddler was a mere boy, a lad who was breathing heavily through blackened, sun-parched lips. His face was drawn and his expression set. The strokes with which he tried to move the canoe nearer to the aircraft were short, and without power. It was plain that he was nearly exhausted.

"Who are you?" called Nigel in English.

Somewhat to his surprise the reply came back in the same language.

"I'm British," called the boy.

Nigel taxied closer. "Where have you just come from?"

"From Italy."

"What were you doing there?"

"I was interned, but I escaped."

"Where do you think you're making for?" demanded Nigel.

"Anywhere," was the reply. "I hoped to reach Malta, if I was not picked up by a British ship."

Nigel smiled grimly. "Stand by. I'm going to take you aboard."

He taxied the Osprey so close that by standing on a float he could help the boy to climb into the machine. "Hold on. I'll get you some water," he said, and reached for his flask.

The boy drank deeply. "My word! That was good," he gasped. "I was about all in. It's pretty hot down here on the open sea."

"What's your name?" inquired Nigel curiously.

"Hubert—Hubert Fairfax," answered the boy. Then he went on quickly. "Please take me to the nearest British headquarters. I have important news. The Italians are building——"

"All right, laddie, save your breath," broke in Nigel. "You can tell your story to the Air Commodore. I'll take you to my base."

"Where is your base?" asked Hubert.

"Malta," returned Nigel. "Sit down and make yourself comfortable. I'll soon have you there."

The Osprey's engine roared. Its floats cut a creamy scar across the tranquil surface of the blue water. The scar ended abruptly as the machine rose into the air, heading south.

Twenty minutes later Hubert was telling his story to an attentive group of British officers at a Maltese marine aircraft base, and a strange story it was.

It seemed that when Mussolini decided to enrich himself at the expense of his neighbours, Hubert's father had been a merchant in Rome. At that time Hubert was only twelve years old—even now he was only fifteen. His father, being a British subject, had been arrested and interned. He himself had been taken away from school, but because he was able to speak and write both English and Italian fluently, the Italians had pressed him to become a Fascist, so that he could work for them in the propaganda department.

At first, naturally, Hubert had refused to do this. Then, thinking the matter over, it struck him that by pretending to meet the wishes of Mussolini's Fascists he might gain their confidence, and so learn of matters of importance—information which, by some means or other, he would convey to his own people.

For a long time nothing had happened—that is, nothing of such supreme importance that an attempt to escape would be justified. But all the time he had wormed his way more and more into the confidence of the Questura, the Italian equivalent of the Nazi Gestapo. Then at last, came the chance for which he had been waiting. He learned that Nazi engineers had arrived from Germany, and had started to build a big secret submarine base, with oil storage tanks, among the limestone cliffs near Casagrande, at no great distance from the internment camp of Castelvero, where his father, and some other British subjects were confined —where he himself was sometimes sent to do translation work for the Commandant, Major Gelmetti.

Hubert had bided his time. He wanted to make sure. But at last there was no longer any doubt. Submarine component parts had been sent from Germany and were being assembled. U-boat commanders had arrived, and the new base was about to begin operations. The Nazis and the Fascists hoped for great things from it. They had predicted confidently that they would prevent any more British ships from getting through to the Middle East. And it seemed to Hubert that this was quite likely if nothing was done about it.

Of the existence of the secret base there was no doubt whatever, declared Hubert. Twice, by night, he had made excursions to Casagrande, and had studied the ground from all angles. On the last occasion he had been rather too ambitious. Securing an old Italian uniform he had gone right in to the base; and had he been content with that all might have been well. But in passing the Commandant's office he had looked through the window, and had seen a map lying on the table. He recognized it as a large scale map of the whole base. The room was empty. It was the chance of a lifetime. In a moment he had entered and secured the map. Unfortunately, just as he was leaving, the Commandant had come back into the room. There was only one thing to do, and that was to make a bolt for it.

Hubert smiled wanly as he narrated his adventures of the next few hours. The general alarm was sounded, but instead of attempting to escape, he had mixed with Fascist soldiers, and had actually helped in the search—for himself. Just before dawn he had slipped away. Only one thought was now in his mind. Escape. Escape from Italy, so that he might pass the precious map into hands that would know how to deal with it. A little way along the coast he had come to a small fishing village. Unable to manage any of the larger vessels alone, he had taken a canoe, and in this he had paddled to a nearby island, where, in a cave under the rocks, he had taken refuge until night came again. As soon as it was dark he had set off, hoping to reach Malta. He had paddled all night, until his hands were raw. Dawn had found him well out to sea, but of a British ship there was no sign. Several times he had seen Italian aircraft, which he had no doubt were looking for him, but he had not been spotted until the Caproni appeared. This would have been the finish had not the British Osprey arrived at the crucial moment, and rescued him. As he finished speaking Hubert took the map from his jacket pocket, and in a buzz of excitement laid it on the desk.

The Air Commodore patted him on the shoulder. "Jolly good show, my boy," he complimented. "It's fellows like you who help the fighting men to win wars. Now you go off and get some sleep while we talk things over."

With this arrangement Hubert was well content, for he was nearer to exhaustion than he would have cared to admit. In five minutes he was sound asleep on Nigel's bed.

Later in the day he was awakened to find three officers standing beside him. One was the Air Commodore. Another was in navy blue. The third was a tall, good looking man, with a firm jaw and bright blue eyes, in khaki battledress.

"Don't move, Hubert. We've come to ask you a few questions," began the Air Commodore. He touched the naval officer on the sleeve. "This, by the way, is Captain Norton; and this,"—he indicated the army officer—"is Colonel Brown. You may have heard of him as the leader of many daring commando raids."

Hubert caught his breath. So *this* was the celebrated Colonel "Buster" Brown of whom he had often heard in Italy, for the record of the Colonel's specially selected warriors, sometimes called "Buster's Bulldogs" was known all along the coast of Europe from Salonica to Marseilles. The commandos had taken their emblem from the nick-name, and every one wore a red bulldog, with teeth bared, on his sleeve.

"I'm proud to meet you, sir," said Hubert. And he meant it. "Can I do something for you?"

A faint smile softened the Colonel's face. "Yes, I think you can," he answered cheerfully. "You brought us the news, so it is only right that you should know we're thinking of having a crack at this new

He taxied the Osprey so close that by standing on a float he could help the boy to climb into the machine.

submarine base. I may as well be frank. A map is a very useful thing; indeed, it would be hazardous to undertake a raid of this sort without one; but still more valuable is a guide, someone who has actually been over the ground. How would you feel about coming on the raid? Your job would be to show us where the things are. Naturally, you wouldn't do any actual fighting."

"Why not?" demanded Hubert.

The Colonel glanced at the other officers and smiled. "You're a bit young for that sort of thing."

"If a gun is held straight it doesn't matter who pulls the trigger," Hubert pointed out.

The Colonel laughed. "All right. You can carry a gun, if that's how you feel about it. But be careful who you shoot. Things are apt to get a bit mixed up, you know, in the dark. May I take it that you will come?"

Hubert hesitated. "There's just one thing, sir," he said.

"What's that?"

"My father is in the internment camp at Castelvero. There are about twenty other Britishers there. The camp is under four miles from the submarine base. Couldn't we rescue him at the same time?"

At first the Colonel looked doubtful. "It might be done," he said slowly. "The main job, of course, would be to destroy the submarine pens, and the oil tanks, but it might be possible to detach a small party from the main force for the express purpose of rescuing the British prisoners. I won't promise, but I'll bear it in mind when I make my plans."

"That's good enough for me, sir," agreed Hubert. "I'll come, anyway. I know every inch of the ground."

205

"Splendid," cried the Colonel.

"When is the raid going to take place, sir?" asked Hubert.

"We're hoping to do it to-night, before the enemy has time to make any alterations, which he may, now that he knows the map has been stolen," replied the Colonel. "If you are coming you had better see the quartermaster about a uniform. If you came in civilian clothes, and were captured, you would be liable to be shot as a spy. Be at my office in an hour, and with the map in front of us we'll go over the ground."

The officers went out, leaving Hubert not quite sure whether this was really happening, or if he was dreaming.

After dressing quickly he went out, and in the barracks adjacent to the aerodrome buildings, found the quartermaster's stores. A number of tall, keen-eyed men were standing about, talking, or resting in the shade. All wore the red bulldog on their shoulders. Never before, thought Hubert, had he seen so many athletic-looking men together. As he approached he heard one of them say: "That must be the kid who got away from Italy—the one Lieutenant Steer picked up this morning."

The quartermaster was waiting, having been warned by headquarters that a recruit was reporting for kit. There was some difficulty in finding a battledress small enough, but in the end, with the help of the regimental tailor, Hubert was accoutred. There were smiles when he asked for a revolver.

"Who are you going to shoot?" asked a lanky, loose-limbed sergeant, after a wink at the quarter-master.

"You'll see," declared Hubert, and marched off to the Colonel's office, where he found a conference between the three services—Navy, Army and Air Force—in progress. He was invited to be seated where he could see the map, and from time to time answered questions concerning footpaths, the state of the ground, the position of barbed wire, and the like. At length he remarked: "If I may say so, I don't think you'll take this place by direct frontal attack."

"Why not?" asked Colonel Brown quickly.

"Because the whole defence system is laid out against attack from the sea," answered Hubert without hesitation.

"How do you know that?" inquired the Colonel.

"Because I overheard two Nazi officers talking about it," replied Hubert.

"But there doesn't seem to be any alternative," observed the Colonel.

"I think there is, sir," argued Hubert respectfully. "If our troops try to storm those cliffs the casualties will be awful. I know the ground and I'm sure of it. If the first attack came from the rear our troops would be on the top of the hill instead of at the bottom. The Nazis would have to turn their guns, and all their equipment, to meet an attack from that direction. And that would take time. Then, if the main attack was launched below, our troops would have a much better chance, and the enemy would find himself between two fires."

The Colonel looked up from the map which he had been studying while Hubert spoke. "I think he's right," he decided. "The only thing is," he went on, looking at Hubert, "how are we going to arrange this first attack from the rear? The troops would have to land on the beach to get in that position."

"Not necessarily, sir," disputed Hubert. "They could be taken in by air."

"You mean, dropped by parachute?"

"Either that, or a machine could land."

"I don't see any possible landing ground," said the Colonel.

"Nevertheless, there is one," declared Hubert. "Close by the internment camp at Castelvero an area of ground has just been cleared to make an emergency runway for the aircraft which will be needed to protect the base against bombing attacks. The British prisoners, my father among them, have been made to do the work. In fact, that is why the internment camp was established there."

"But I don't understand why this landing ground hasn't been spotted by our reconnaissance aircraft," put in the Air Commodore.

"The reason is, no doubt, because it is perfectly camouflaged," replied Hubert. "There are trees, rocks, and even cottages, but they are all canvas and paint."

"Well—well. We *are* learning something," said the Air Commodore. "But if the camouflage is as perfect as that, it would be asking too much to expect one of our pilots to find the place at night."

"I could find it," said Hubert quickly.

"You mean, you'd go over with the pilot?"

"Better still, sir, I'd go down by parachute and show a light at the southern end of the runway. The aircraft could then land over me."

"Aren't you being rather venturesome?" put in the Colonel drily.

"What does it matter, if I can do it—and I think I can," answered Hubert.

"How far is this landing ground from the submarine base?"

"About three miles, sir. As soon as the troops were on the ground I could lead them to it."

The three officers looked at each other.

"Of course, if that could be done, it would be the answer to all our problems," asserted the Colonel.

"But we couldn't get more than a dozen men into one aircraft," the Air Commodore pointed out. "I doubt if that would be enough to make much of a show. They might be wiped out before the landing party could get ashore."

"I can give you the answer to that, sir," stated Hubert. "There are twenty tough Britishers in the internment camp. We could take spare weapons in the machine, capture the camp, and arm the prisoners. That would give us a striking force of more than thirty men. The prisoners would be glad of a chance to fight, particularly if they knew that they would be picked up afterwards, with the troops, and taken to Malta."

The Colonel looked round the table. "There is sound common sense in what the boy says," he declared. "I propose that we lay our plans on those lines."

And so it was agreed.

At ten o'clock that night, feeling awkward in his cumbersome parachute, Hubert stood on a darkened aerodrome watching twelve selected commandos file into a Bombay troop carrier. Two cases of rifles, with boxes of ammunition and hand grenades, had

209

already been put aboard. Leader of the "Bulldog" detachment was the tall, lanky sergeant, whom Hubert had seen in the quartermaster's office. He grinned cheerfully at Hubert as he passed. "You're starting young, aren't you?" he inquired.

"Why not?" replied Hubert.

"I hear you're going to show us the way?"

"That's right," agreed Hubert.

"You'd better keep close to me," advised the sergeant.

"I shan't go far away you may be sure," returned Hubert, smiling.

The others laughed.

The pilot appeared. He was Lieutenant Nigel Steer, the officer who had that morning rescued Hubert from the sea. "It seems I let myself in for something when I fished you out of the drink, my lad," he greeted cheerfully. "Come on. Let's get aboard. It's time we were off."

They climbed into the cockpit and settled themselves in their seats. The engines roared. The control signal flashed, and the big machine raced across the aerodrome like an arrow. Another minute and it was in the air, heading out over the starlit sea.

The distance to the objective was a hundred and sixty miles, and the Bombay covered it at cruising speed, without incident, in just under an hour—the period allowed for the flight. The whole operation had, Hubert knew, been carefully timed to the minute. The main assault from the sea was to be launched at half an hour past midnight, which meant that the airborne commandos had one and a half hours to do their work at the internment camp, amd make the feint attack from the steep hill overlooking the submarine base.

Hubert stiffened as the pilot pointed at a long black shadow that lay asprawl the northern horizon. "Italy," he said, quietly, and Hubert studied the coastline intently to pick up his position.

"There's a village straight ahead," he said. "If we fly over it we shall be heard. There's a long stretch of deserted coast a little father to the north; it would be better to cross there, I think."

"And having crossed, how far is it to the landing ground?" asked Nigel.

"About four miles."

"Good. We ought to be able to reach it from here, so I'll cut the motors."

The noise of the engines died away to a sullen mutter. The nose of the big machine tilted down, and in that position ran parallel with the enemy coast, which showed no more signs of life than a desert.

"This is the place—turn in here," advised Hubert, who was staring down at the deeply indented shore.

The noise of the engines died way altogether, and the aircraft crept across the coast like a shadow. The shining sea now lay behind, and sombre land ahead.

Hubert's eyes probed the darkness, picking up familiar landmarks. "A little more to the left," he guided. "A little more . . . little more . . . steady! Hold her there. You're heading straight for the runway." He got up.

"Have you ever jumped before?" asked Nigel.

"Never—but I had some instruction on the aero-drome this afternoon," answered Hubert. "I count three, then pull the ring."

"That's right."

"As soon as I'm on the ground I shall go straight to the runway," went on Hubert. "When you see my flash, long and short strokes alternately, you'll know I'm standing at the northern end of the landing ground. If you come in over me, heading south, you'll have plenty of room in front of you. Ignore everything you see on the ground—it's only camouflage."

"Right you are," agreed Nigel.

Hubert opened the door. "See you later," he said, and gripping the parachute release ring, plunged into the void.

There was a moment of confusion while he counted one—two—three, and then pulled the ring. An instant later, pressure on his harness told him that the parachute had opened. Glancing up he saw it billowing over him like a gigantic mushroom. It was a strange sensation, but not in the least what he expected. There was no feeling of falling. His paramount impression was one of awful loneliness. He seemed to be the only person in the world. The only sound was the faint hum of the aircraft passing through the air, but he could no longer see it.

For some minutes he appeared to get no closer to the ground, and an unpleasant feeling swept over him that he was suspended in space with no means of getting down. He had ample time to take careful note of his relative position with the runway, and he saw that he would alight close to it, if not actually on it. Then, suddenly, the earth seemed to rush up at him, and he bent his knees, as he had been told, to take the shock of landing. His feet struck the ground, and he fell, but he was up again in a moment, with the silk settling gently round him. Pushing it clear he slipped out of his harness and felt for his torch. For a few seconds he stood still, listening intently, but no sound came out of the darkness, so he set off at a run for the northern end of the landing ground, which was about two hundred paces distant. Reaching it, slightly breathless with excitement, he held his torch vertical, and flashed the prearranged signal. For a time nothing happened, and he was just beginning to wonder if Nigel had lost him when a faint hum came from the silence overhead. He continued to send the signal, and a few seconds later he saw the black bulk of the aircraft coming towards him from the north. He threw himself flat as the dark shape swept low over him; as soon as it had passed he was on his feet again, racing after it. By the time he had reached the spot where it had stopped, the troops were out, lined up as if for parade. Each man helped to carry the spare weapons and ammunition.

This, now, was the plan. The aircraft was to remain on the ground while the attack was made on the internment camp, and the party had moved on to the submarine base. The idea of this was, if the scheme went wrong, the aircraft would provide a way of escape, but provided all went well the machine would return home, empty, at the discretion of the pilot. In accordance with this arrangement Hubert said good-bye to Nigel and took his place at the head of the file of troops, for it was his task to lead them to the camp.

"I'm ready when you are," he told the sergeant.

"Lead on, my lucky lad," was the reply, and the file moved forward, like a line of ghosts, into the night.

During the walk that followed Hubert had his first experience of what training could do in the art of stealth. Although there were twelve men behind him, heavily armed and loaded with equipment, they made no sound, and more than once he looked behind him to make sure that they were still there. After covering a good distance in this manner he stopped, and addressed the sergeant. "The camp is just in front of us," he said. "It is surrounded by a barbed wire fence ten feet high and four feet thick. Sentries patrol the wire. The entrance, with the guardhouse, is about a hundred paces to the right. The hut that holds the prisoners is in the middle of the compound."

"Good!" said the sergeant. "Leave this to me."

He beckoned two Bulldogs forward, and sent one to the left and the other to the right. "They'll take care of any sentries that come along," he muttered grimly. Selecting another man, armed with a Tommy gun, to go with him, he invited Hubert to lead the way to the wire. By the time they had reached it the sergeant's massive wire cutters were in his hand. There was a faint *snick*, and the first strand of wire parted. The snicks were repeated as the sergeant cut a clear path right through the fence, carefully drawing aside each strand of wire as it was severed.

"That's it," said the sergeant when the way was clear. "Lead on to the hut."

"What about the rest of the fellows?" asked Hubert.

"They'll stay here and cover our retreat in case there's an alarm. Tell me, is there a guard in the hut?"

"Three soldiers, usually a corporal and two privates, sleep in a cubicle at the end," explained Hubert.

214

"They have the keys of the hut, but there is a door that leads from their room to the prisoner's quarters."

"We'll deal with the guards first," said the sergeant confidently. "Lead on."

With a strange sensation of unreality Hubert led the way across the dusty compound. He had trodden the ground many times before, but never had he imagined returning in such circumstances as these. As the dark outline of the long hutment loomed up his heart began to beat faster, but he kept his feelings under control. Moving cautiously now, he made his way to the end of the hut. "Here is the door," he whispered. "The Italians are inside. They must be awake," he added, indicating a chink of light that edged a window.

What happened next occurred with such speed that Hubert was petrified. It was almost as though the sergeant had rehearsed the very act over and over again. Drawing his revolver, he rapped sharply on the door with the butt. It was opened from inside, and the figure of an Italian soldier stood outlined against the lighted interior. The sergeant thrust the muzzle of the revolver into his face.

"Get back and don't make a sound," he snapped.

The Italian's hand dropped to his belt, and he drew in his breath sharply as if to cry out. This may have been purely instinctive, or the result of shock, but either way it was unfortunate for him. There was a vicious smack as the sergeant's fist flew out; it took the Italian on the point of the jaw, and he reeled backwards into the room to finish in a heap on the floor. By that time the sergeant was inside, with his revolver, as menacing as the head of a cobra about to strike, covering two Italians, a private and a corporal, who sat at a small table playing cards. With eyes as wide as saucers, and jaws sagging in consternation and surprise, they stared at the sergeant. Neither moved.

Said the sergeant to Hubert: "Tell them if they make one sound it will be their last. If they keep their mouths shut no harm will come to them."

Hubert passed on this information, speaking in Italian. There was no need to repeat it. The Italians did not move. Nor did they speak. They just sat and stared, as if hypnotized.

"Get the keys, laddie," ordered the sergeant.

Still speaking in Italian Hubert demanded the keys, and the corporal passed them over without a word. The sergeant took them and unlocked the inner door. The room beyond was in darkness. "Hello, there!" he called.

There was a sudden stirring in the gloom. "Who is it?" asked a voice.

"British commandos," replied the sergeant. "We've come to fetch you. Get your kit together. Make it snappy—but don't make a noise."

Sounds of feverish activity, and a buzz of conversation, came from inside the hut.

Hubert spoke into the darkness. "Is my father there? This is Hubert Fairfax speaking."

There was a low cry inside the but, and a bearded man, in canvas trousers and sandals, appeared in the doorway. "Hubert!" he gasped.

"Hello, Father," said Hubert calmly, with difficulty controlling his emotion. "Make haste, please. I'm acting as guide, and we have other work to do. We can talk later."

216

In five minutes the prisoners announced that they were ready.

The sergeant spoke to Hubert. "Tell these fellows that I'm going to lock them in. If they want to go on living they had better stay inside and keep quiet."

Hubert translated, and the Italians went into the hut vacated by the prisoners. They made no protest. The door was locked and the sergeant led the way to the gap in the wire, where contact was made with the troops who had remained there. Speaking in a low voice he explained his mission to the released prisoners, after which the spare weapons were distributed.

"What about starting with the troops in the barracks, here?" suggested a small, sandy-haired Scot. "That cranky Fascist Gelmetti had me flogged the other day because I was sick with fever and didn't work hard enough to please him."

The sergeant shook his head. "Sorry, pal. If we start a rumpus here the main plan may go wrong. While things are quiet it's our job to leave them like that. There'll be plenty of rough work presently, if I know anything about it. We're a minute behind schedule, so it's time we were moving towards the submarine base. Lead on, youngster. You're doing fine."

Hubert resumed his position at the head of the file and set off at a steady pace towards the sea.

The sergeant joined him. "How long will it take us to get there?" he asked.

"If all goes well, we should cover the distance in three quarters of an hour," answered Hubert.

"Good enough," said the sergeant. "No more talking now."

Like a line of lost spirits the commandos moved across the deserted landscape.

Hubert's intimate knowledge of the country was now of immense value, as he himself was able to realize. Without a guide, the progress of the troops would have been much slower; as it was, not only was he able to avoid human habitations—small farmhouses, and the like—but he could lessen the distance by taking short cuts direct across country, at the same time using the cover provided by olive groves, vineyards, and fields of maize. In this way the party made good progress, and came within sight of the sea in five minutes under the estimated time. The sergeant raised his hand and the party halted. There was something uncanny about the way things happened, how orders were obeyed, without a word being spoken.

Cupping his hands round his mouth the sergeant breathed into Hubert's ear. "How far are we from the base?"

Hubert answered in like manner. "It's immediately below the crest of the low hill in front of us. The wire runs round the top of the hill. The actual distance to the oil storage tanks is about four hundred paces."

"Will you take me forward to where I can have a good look at the place?" suggested the sergeant.

"Yes," answered Hubert. "There are sentries, don't forget."

The sergeant turned. A whisper passed along the line and the commandos sank to the ground. They seemed to melt into the earth. The ex-prisoners followed their example. This done the sergeant tapped Hubert on the arm. "Let's go," he breathed.

Hubert moved forward into the darkness. Now that he was on the fringe of the danger zone he was quite calm, which was queer, because his brain was racing, and his muscles felt taut, vibrating, like elastic. He seemed to walk on air, hardly conscious of his limbs. Beside him moved the long, lean sergeant, slightly bent, like a steel spring ready to snap.

They reached the wire just as a sentry materialized out of the surrounding gloom. They were directly in his path, so there was no escape. He saw them. His rifle moved swiftly, the bayonet gleaming like dull ice in the starlight. He lunged. But the sergeant had moved with the speed of light. His body twisted. As the bayonet slid past his side he seized the muzzle of the rifle with his left hand and jerked it forward, pulling the man with it. There was a grunt as the sergeant's knee drove into the sentry's stomach. His revolver went up, and came down with a thud. The Italian slumped to the ground like a coat slipping from a peg.

"Okay," breathed the sergeant. "I reckon he'll stay quiet for a bit."

Hubert moistened his lips, which had turned dry, and moved forward. Again came the *snick—snick —snick* as the sergeant's wire cutters came into action. They crawled through the gap, and looked down on the several miscellaneous buildings that formed the submarine base. Hubert pointed them out—the headquarters office, the machine shops, the oil depots, the staff hutments and the U-boat pens. A few lights were showing; a motor hummed, and sounds of metal on metal suggested that work was in progress.

"That's all I want to see," whispered the sergeant,

219

and backed away through the gap in the wire to where the Bulldogs were waiting. To these he gave terse and concise instructions, and Hubert's nerves tingled as the troops prepared for action. Straps were tightened; hand grenades were loosened, and Tommy guns were raised. The whole party then moved forward through the gap, and under the sergeant's directions the men took up their positions.

Hubert had now played his part, and there was nothing more he could do. He could only lie in the sparse, sun-dried grass, and wait. Presently the sergeant joined him. Lying at full length he looked at his luminous wrist watch.

"Two minutes to zero hour," he said softly.

They were the longest two minutes Hubert had ever known. Silence reigned. Stars sparkled, unmindful of the affairs of men. Somewhere not far away a sea bird uttered its plaintive cry. Hubert found the nerve strain almost intolerable. He wondered vaguely what would happen next.

Again the sergeant looked at his watch. "One minute to go," he observed.

The atmosphere was now brittle with expectancy. It struck Hubert as odd that such desperate operations should be cut into minutes and seconds, and he said as much.

"Perfect timing is everything, even on a routine job like this," remarked the sergeant casually.

Routine job, thought Hubert. That was what the sergeant called it. He wondered what a major operation would be like. "What had I better do?" he asked.

"You can't stay up here because we're not coming back this way; if you did you'd get left behind," answered the sergeant. "You'd better stay close behind me. Keep your head down when the stuff starts flying. Well, here we go." The sergeant stood erect and whistled softly.

As if by magic the line of men rose from the ground, and in silence, without undue haste, advanced towards the submarine depot like a reluctant wave. Hubert walked behind the sergeant, who was carrying a Tommy gun at his right hip. For a moment or two nothing happened. It was unreal, uncanny. Why didn't somebody do something? Hubert experienced an almost irresistable desire to shout. The buildings became more clearly defined. Beyond them the placid sea shimmered to the stars. Beside a mole, a long grey shape that was obviously a submarine, lay like a sleeping crocodile.

Suddenly the sergeant, who was slightly in the lead, stumbled, and then paused to disengage his legs from a strand of wire. Simultaneously a bell jangled harshly among the buildings. There was a shout of alarm, followed by a volley of orders.

"Trip wire! That's torn it," said the sergeant calmly. "Now for the fireworks. Hold your hat, laddie." As he finished speaking the sergeant put a whistle to his lips and blew three shrill blasts.

The effect was stunning. From all along the line of advancing Bulldogs sprang a fringe of fire, and the dreadful music of war shattered the silence. The crackle of machine guns was a continuous roll, so that the air vibrated with the noise of it. Tracer bullets flashed. Grenades thundered. Star shells soared into the sky, to shed an unnatural incandescent glare over the scene.

The Bulldogs did not stop. They did not run.

221

They kept steadily on, in line, as if on parade, pouring before them a deadly hail of lead. It was as though an avalanche of death was rolling down the hill. In the base itself all seemed to be in confusion. Men were running, shouting. Doors banged. Whistles blew. A siren wailed horribly, adding to the uproar. Flecks of orange flame stabbed the darkness, and bullets began to tear furrows in the turf, or whistle through the ranks of the Bulldogs. Some glanced off the rocks, and ricochetted, screaming. Fearful though it was, Hubert's blood tingled with the excitement of the battle. The Nazis had started it; now they were getting it back. That was as it should be. He saw men fall, but, strangely enough, it did not occur to him that he might be the next.

"Keep in line there!" shouted the sergeant, to some of the Bulldogs who were beginning to forge ahead.

Of the next ten minutes Hubert had only confused impressions. The Bulldogs had now reached the boundary of the base itself. The oil storage tanks loomed like great beehives. The sergeant, who seemed to Hubert to be exposing himself recklessly, took a bomb from his belt, dragged the pin out with his teeth, and hurled it at the nearest tank. The missile exploded in a sheet of flame and hurtling metal. Then came a dreadful sight. The tank, pierced by bomb splinters, began to leak; the oil took fire, and a stream of flame poured towards the submarine pens, lighting the scene with a lurid glow. On the deck of the submarine men were working furiously, evidently in the hope of getting the U-boat away before the flames reached it. The forward gun came into action. Shells screamed; but the shooting was wild, and they burst far beyond the Bulldogs.

Hubert could see the enemy plainly now, but there seemed to be no order in their behaviour. Pandemonium reigned. Nevertheless, some groups of men were formed, and they surged towards the attacking force. The sergeant's Tommy gun chattered. Men fell. Others came on. The shape of their helmets revealed them to be Nazis. More men appeared, some only half dressed.

The two forces met. Hubert tried hard to keep near the sergeant, but he tripped over something, stumbled and fell. As he scrambled to his feet a pistol blazed almost in his face and he went over backwards. He found himself looking up at a grim-faced, square-headed Nazi officer. The German's lips parted, showing his teeth, as he pointed an automatic; but a rifle butt crashed on his head, and he fell across Hubert who, panting with shock, pushed the body aside and regained his feet.

The scene was now fearful to behold. Several of the oil tanks were ablaze. One, apparently containing petrol, blew up. Rivers of fire trickled between the huts. Fires sprang up everywhere. Even the sea was on fire. It was as light as day. Hubert could not see the sergeant, but he made out a small group of Bulldogs standing back to back fighting an overwhelming number of Nazis. Nazis were everywhere. There were over two hundred of them in the camp, Hubert remembered. The position seemed to be getting desperate.

Then a new sound, a mighty roar, rose high above the din of battle. It was cheering. For a moment Hubert did not understand. Dazed by the noise, and the speed of events, he had forgotten all about the main force of Bulldogs, under Colonel Buster

Brown. Then he saw them, leaping on a mole from long rakish motor boats, at the far end of the base, the only area of water free from burning oil. The enemy saw them too, and as Hubert had foreseen, were at once thrown into confusion. Attacked from two sides, confusion soon gave way to chaos. From that moment the result of the battle was no longer in doubt.

Then Hubert saw the lanky sergeant, fighting like a madman, near the door of the headquarters building which, being of concrete, had not taken fire. He raced towards him. A Nazi seemed to come from nowhere, with bayonet lowered, to intercept him. Hubert fired his revolver for the first time, and was astonished to see the German sprawl face downwards on the ground. By the time he reached the sergeant the Nazis were falling back.

"Hello, where have you been?" greeted the sergeant. "I told you to stay with me."

"I tried to," muttered Hubert.

The sergeant grinned. He was in a dreadful state. His uniform was covered with oil and filth; his collar seemed to be twisted round the back of his neck; he had lost his steel helmet, and his hair was plastered on his face with sweat.

"We've got 'em on the run," declared the sergeant, as he coolly surveyed the scene.

This was obviously true. The commandos were arriving in increasing numbers. There were bursts of wild cheering. The Germans and Italians who had escaped annihilation were either in flight, or stood with their hands up. Some who had taken to the hills were being pursued by Bulldogs. The submarine was sinking by the bows, although how this had happened Hubert did not know. Slowly, like a tempest that blows itself out, the din subsided. The sergeant lit a cigarette and blew a cloud of smoke into the air.

"You'd better see if you can find your father," he told Hubert. "I shall have to stay here to guard this place." He pointed to the enemy headquarters. "There ought to be some useful documents in there."

"I haven't seen my father since the show began," said Hubert.

"I spotted him a minute or two ago, down there by the mole," returned the sergeant.

Hubert went on towards the mole. On the way he met Colonel Brown, with his staff officers.

"Hello, my boy," said the Colonel. "I'm glad to see you're still on your feet. Things were pretty lively for a little while. Well, it's all over bar the demolition work. Did you get your father, and the other fellows, out of the internment camp?"

"Yes, sir," answered Hubert. "I'm looking for him now. I think I can see him on the mole."

"Run along, then. I'm busy now." The Colonel walked on.

Hubert ran down to the mole, where the wounded were being mustered. Medical officers and orderlies were working swiftly, efficiently. Stretcher bearers were helping the wounded into the boats. Hubert's father was having an arm bandaged.

"It's only a scratch," he made haste to assure Hubert.

"Get aboard, please," ordered a naval officer. "We shall soon be clearing out."

Feeling limp from reaction Hubert found a seat in a boat beside his father and watched the scene

225

ashore—a scene of efficient activity. Wounded men were still being brought in. Engineers were moving about, some with ominous looking parcels, others unwinding spools of wire. Then a bugle rang out clear and high, and everyone began to converge on the boats. As each craft received its full compliment, it backed away, and a convoy began to form off-shore.

Hubert suddenly became aware that he was tired. And he was, in fact, dozing, when his father touched him on the arm.

"All the boats are away," he said. "Watch this—it should be worth watching."

A whistle shrilled. An instant later sheet after sheet of flame leapt high into the air, while the air rocked, and the water heaved, with the force of the explosions.

"I don't think the Nazis will use *that* base for some time," said an engineer officer, who was sitting close to Hubert.

"That's the finish, eh?" murmured Hubert.

"Yes, that's the finish," was the quiet answer.

Engines throbbed, and the raiding boats, in a close convoy, stood out to sea. Overhead, the Bombay aircraft droned homewards. Suddenly Hubert started and peered forward into the gloom. A long low craft was racing across their bows. A similar shape was coming up on the left; another on the right.

"What are those ships?" asked Hubert, with a twinge of alarm.

"They're our escorting destroyers," replied the naval officer in charge of the boat.

Hubert sighed his relief, and with his head against his father's shoulder, fell asleep.

226

When he opened his eyes, dawn was staining the east with pink. He sat up abruptly, realizing that some noise had awakened him. Lifting up his eyes he saw a squadron of planes overhead, in open formation. His frown of alarm turned to a smile when he saw the familiar ring markings of the Royal Air Force. For a moment he had thought they might be enemy aircraft.

The lanky sergeant, in the next boat, saw him and waved. He pointed to the destroyers, the aircraft, and the weary Bulldogs. "Quite a party," he called. "How are you feeling?"

"Fine," answered Hubert. "It all went like clockwork.

"That's as it should be, on these routine ops," said the sergeant. "You ought to come with us on a really big job."

"This one," declared Hubert emphatically, "was big enough for me—thank you."

His father touched him on the arm and pointed to a long purple stain on the horizon. "Malta," he said. "We're nearly home. What a night it's been."

"According to the Bulldogs," murmured Hubert, "it was only a routine operation."

THE END